I0581121

Books by Julie Midnight

<u>Monstrous Hearts</u>

Wolf's Wife
Wolf's Bane
Wolf's Kin

Wolf's Wife

MONSTROUS HEARTS
BOOK ONE

Julie Midnight

ISBN: 978-1-7367836-0-3 (Paperback)

Front cover image by Julie Midnight
Book design by Daniel Young

Printed by Kindle Direct Publishing in the United States

First Printing Edition 2021

Hellcat Press LLC
www.hellcatpressllc.com

Table of Contents

CHAPTER ONE

The Cabin

The cabin was rundown, dusty, and cold from the wind whistling through the cracks and gaps in its walls, and Alice winced while setting her luggage on the bed. The bags bulged with more than enough clothes for the month-long trip—a trip that would likely prove as miserable as every other they had tried in the past five years.

Magdalene already smoked, running a hand through her thick, brown hair while staring out the window at the bristling fir and redwood. "Jesus, what a place. This is supposed to be a retreat?"

"It's not too late to try Tahoe instead. We'd get there before sunset."

"Fuck that. It'll be seething with tourists. I need quiet."

The light from the winter sun, dim and sickly as it was, transformed the features of Magdalene's face into the transcendent purity that had first drawn Alice to her. Alice fell still, watching. Moments like these were precious, burned into her brain to be later pulled out and treasured like a string of pearls released from a locked jewelry box.

Then Magdalene shifted, and the play of light across her face changed, revealing the flatness in her dark eyes and the sullen set to her mouth.

Alice swallowed a sigh and slipped over to hug her from behind, fingers sinking into the thick, woolen coat the other woman wore. When Magdalene didn't react, she said, "We both agreed it'd be good to get away and recharge without anything to distract us. Somewhere rustic and peaceful."

"It won't work."

Alice hesitated. A familiar tightness appeared in her belly at the knowledge that nothing she said could hold the right words. "Maybe it'll help. The last short story you started before we came here was very—"

"It was shit." With a rough shrug of her shoulders, Magdalene knocked her hands away. Then she brushed by with an exhalation of smoke. "You better get some wood for a fire. This place is freezing."

Tears prickled at Alice's eyes as she nodded.

The warmth and brightness of flames did nothing to lighten the mood. Clouds swelled in the sky, bringing about an early evening and a steady rain. After unpacking, Alice found a battered pot in the kitchen cabinet and began cooking with the groceries they had brought with them—*coq au vin*, the original recipe halved since Magdalene only ever picked at food. When

Alice tried opening a bottle of pinot noir, the cork broke. She swore.

"Here."

She hadn't even heard Magdalene approach, but there she was, taking the corkscrew and putting it to work on a second bottle of wine. When the cork pulled out with a neat pop, Alice smiled at her.

Magdalene didn't smile back. Instead, she took the first bottle and returned to the fireplace, corkscrew still in hand.

Alice felt her expression freeze. "Magdalene…"

"I'm not getting shitfaced. Just need something against the cold."

And from there, Magdalene remained in front of the hearth, feeding it the occasional log while she stared at the flames and drank straight from the bottle. Unflinching even when sparks snapped. She was still dressed for the city, in a sleek sweater dress and sleeker boots, but from the hollow grief on her face, one would think she'd come straight from a funeral.

Alice used more force than necessary while chopping the carrots. She wished she could put the knife to that certain medal in its understated case back home. Its arrival was when Magdalene's life had gone sour, and therefore when hers had as well. In the first year after Magdalene tried following up *The Chrysalis*, she had been wry about her struggles. Yet things weren't as simple as the pressure of a prestigious debut novel crushing the delicate bones of whatever story followed it.

Magdalene wasn't that simple. More waited beneath the surface, and Alice caught only glimpses.

When half the bottle was gone, Magdalene spoke up. "I can't finish anything, that's the problem. There's something broken in my head, and the story doesn't stand a chance."

Alice had to close her eyes at the sound of her voice. It was easy to remember how Magdalene would whisper words in her ear, once upon a time during the early days of their relationship, transforming the interior of Alice's plain, little mind into landscapes of sound and imagery. She'd felt overwhelmed by Magdalene's bright, strange presence. In awe, even. She'd also been nineteen and very, very silly.

"I turned into the great literary cliche. A has-been. If I were a character in one of my stories, I'd call bullshit on the predictable arc. But I better follow through at this point and commit suicide at forty."

Then Magdalene turned from the fire and smiled at Alice. It was a quick twitch of her lips, as erratic and dangerous as an exposed live wire. "You're stuck with me eleven more years. Poor Alice."

Alice couldn't bring herself to respond.

"Maybe I'll drown myself. Nothing so dramatic as a bridge jump or an overturned boat. No, I'd put stones in my pockets until the fabric threatened to rip. Until I could barely walk to the water's edge. I'd like it to be a pond or a lake. Calm waters to play at my hair, not currents battering me featureless on river rocks. I can't decide on a suicide note, though. A good one will only further tantalize the sense of mystery. But since I can't write for shit, anymore..."

"I hate it when you're like this." Then Alice winced, biting her tongue much too late. It was never wise to give a writer more ammunition. Especially a drunk one.

"I know." The flickering light changed the color of Magdalene's eyes. They looked a vivid honey one moment and black as pitch the next.

When she took another drink from the bottle, Alice tensed. Such a pause meant words were being honed, fine-tuned to the syllable for maximum effect. Regardless of what had broken in Magdalene's mind following the success of her first novel, the remnants remained razor-sharp.

"You want to be someone's wife. We could have done anything when we first arrived. Take a walk in the woods. Explore the cabin to see the podunk decor left by your grandma. Fuck in front of the fire to get warm. But no. You put away clothes and go into the kitchen to make dinner. Is there apple pie for afterward?"

Alice kept her voice calm. "There wasn't enough time."

"Maybe tomorrow." Magdalene faced the fire again.

"Maybe." Then Alice sighed, quietly so that only she would hear it.

Later that night, Magdalene tried to write. She didn't say so, but Alice heard her in the attic, the ceiling creaking and shifting with footsteps while Alice ate alone.

She went to bed alone, too, wrapped up in thermal pajamas and still needing to pull a musty, hand-stitched quilt up to her chin to feel any sort of warmth. The moon was a small, cold jewel in the sky. Alice stared at it while Magdalene's muttering drifted down to her.

Some might say that creatives, the true ones, concern themselves with life in the way of taking coarse clay and fashioning it into art. The base urges of food and shelter are the same as for a beast. Too low, these goals, for hierophants preoccupied with the mysteries of humanity. And to reach arcane heights only to fall again to the level of apes picking themselves—unthinkable.

There in bed, Alice thought of occasional snide references tossed her way about being a trust fund baby, and wondered if financial stability played a larger part in why Magdalene stayed than she'd ever admit. A prestigious novelist didn't become a warehouse worker or salon stylist afterward. It wasn't part of the character arc.

As for why she stayed with Magdalene... Alice couldn't answer that. Any response she scraped up was an excuse, not a reason.

It's not right to leave just because her shining career burned down to embers...

Someone has to look after her...

She loves me...

Old thoughts rolling like marbles through well-worn tracks in her mind, clacking against each other on sleepless nights.

A few minutes past one, Magdalene's footsteps stopped. Alice didn't expect her to appear; more likely, she had passed out from exhaustion or drink, and Alice would lie there alone until the sky grew grey enough to be called morning.

Restless, skin prickling at the thought of so many dark hours to wait through, she threw aside the covers and shuffled to the window. Her reflection waited in the glass, but she ignored it, already aware of what it would show. A girl of twenty-four, wholesome in the face, sturdy in the body, and dead in the heart. Fingers gripping the cold sill, she looked out at a landscape still dripping from the day's rain. The moon hung between lingering clouds, full enough to cast the ground and trees in stark contrast.

Alice wasn't sure how long she stood there, steaming the windowpane with her breath to draw patterns with a finger, before a flicker outside caught her eye. Something moved between shaggy trunks and low-hanging branches, careful on its rangy limbs.

Alice had seen coyotes nosing about the rolling oak savannah where she'd grown up. And if they weren't seen, they were heard, their piercing yelps and screams turning the night into an otherland. This creature wasn't a coyote. It was larger, blunter, more powerful. Alone and silent. A wolf.

The wolf slipped onto a gravel pathway that ran near the cabin before trailing off into the gloom of the forest. Alice watched it nose around the sword ferns and crawling groundcover. It looked like a shadow, dark fur tipped with silver whenever it moved in reach of the moonlight.

Suddenly, the wolf fell still and turned to her, the direction of its muzzle clear. Alice froze. She was seeing things, surely. Canids noticed with their noses first. Locked away in the cabin, she should have been invisible to it. A shiver went over her skin when the wolf took a hesitant step closer and continued to watch her, ears pricked in her direction.

A cold touch at the back of Alice's neck sent her spinning away from the window, breath choking off in a gasp.

Magdalene made an apologetic noise, weaving slightly with one hand still outstretched toward Alice. "You all right?"

Alice's heart pounded against her ribs as she glanced down and saw Magdalene had taken off her shoes. One of those ritualistic quirks that writers held in their tool bag. Once, she'd thought it endearing, a glimpse of childlike superstition in an otherwise humorless line of work. "I didn't hear you come in."

"I'm sorry."

"You startled me, that's all."

"I'm still sorry. About everything." Magdalene reached out and traced the shape of Alice's lips. "You could say so many terrible things about me, and each one would be true. But you're silent as a saint. Always."

The words no longer soothed the hurt like they used to, and Alice gave them nothing more than a nod. "You better come to bed. That wine was potent. I felt it just from eating dinner."

Even drunk, Magdalene moved with grace, her fingers finding the buttons on Alice's pajama top and undoing them with the reverent motion of candles being lit for prayer. "You're my second heart, as fucking cliche as it sounds."

Weariness settled deep in Alice's bones while the fabric slid away and bared her full, heavy breasts. Even so, Magdalene's lips coaxed her to arch into that clever tongue, usually so poisonous, but now sweet and devoted.

When Magdalene's cheek rested against the sensitive skin over Alice's sternum, Alice felt the wetness of tears. "I need you."

Alice herself remained dry-eyed, hand slow as she stroked Magdalene's hair. "I'm here."

CHAPTER TWO

The Pelt

The next morning, Magdalene slouched over the unsteady kitchen table while Alice made the usual hangover breakfast: four slices of toast and a mug of hot water with two wedges of lemon bobbing in it.

When Alice set the plate before her, Magdalene stopped rubbing her eyes long enough to look. "Where's the honey?"

Alice returned to toasting her bagel. She would have liked a fried egg on it but knew the smell would chase Magdalene out of the room. "I forgot to bring some and there isn't any in the cabinets. We'll have to go shopping. Unless you won't do this again while we're here..."

"We'll leave after I finish." Then Magdalene bit into a slice, the resulting crunch an effective period to their conversation.

The nearest town was Perry, a glimmer of civilization among the thick forest, its population of 1,800 spread out in modest homes and local businesses. From the cabin, it was a ten-mile trip on the highway, since all the back roads were flooded from rain or churned up into useless mud.

Magdalene drove, having insisted the threat of vehicular manslaughter would better clear her head over feeling carsick in the passenger seat. Alice had handed over the keys and now kept her mouth tightly shut while staring out the window.

The morning sky looked grey and grim, but the rain had stopped long enough for the puddles on the side of the road to turn back into gravel and grass. Aside from the occasional car, she found no signs of other people. Just looming fir trees and jagged slopes of earth that rose and fell in the distance.

Then—a flash of movement. A dark shape lunged onto the road in front of them. Alice's heart leapt into her throat. "Look out!"

Magdalene swore, cigarette falling from her mouth while she wrenched the wheel. The car's tires skidded on the wet asphalt, but they stopped in time for Alice to see what they had nearly hit. A bear escaped to the other side of the road, its lurching run almost comical.

Alice sat there, panting while Magdalene fumbled for the cigarette. The sound of baying dogs grew clear. So did the flash of oncoming headlights.

"Oh, my God," she said, voice cracking while the first of several coonhounds burst from the trees and leapt onto the road, furious and focused.

Brakes squealed. Alice squeezed her eyes shut, but nothing could keep her from hearing the dog scream. By the time she unbuckled the seatbelt and jumped out, the other car had swerved to a halt, blood and hair stuck in its front grille while it sat askew, one back wheel lodged in the muddy ditch that ran along the side of the road. There was a family inside, the mother and father both twisted in their seats to check the children, but Alice's focus jumped back to the coonhound. It had collapsed on the road, rust-colored fur already stained with a darker red. She saw the frightened whites of the dog's eyes and then heard its whining. It had survived.

Heart pounding, she crouched beside the hound, taking care to keep away from those teeth. Hurt animals were frightened animals, and frightened animals bit. The dog's sides rose in quick, shallow breaths, and Alice could see the bright red of its gums. Early stages of shock. "Magdalene! Get a blanket from the backseat."

When Magdalene didn't reply, Alice risked glancing away from the dog and found her still in the driver's seat, face pale while she stared at the other car. Alice got the blanket herself and ran back.

Other cars appeared on the road from either direction, slowing when the drivers grew unsure. A few simply maneuvered around and continued on, but one, a battered camper van, pulled to the side and waited, the rough idle of its engine adding to the chaos.

Alice, aware of the increasing danger of being run over herself, yelled at Magdalene again. "Help me move him off the road!"

When Magdalene's gaze found her, eyes flat and hard, Alice knew she was still lost, reliving memories in her head. A motorcycle roared by, its tires feet away from Alice and the dog. Alice tried once more, fear adding a ragged note to her voice. "Please!"

The rumble of an engine sent her flinching, but it was only the same van she'd seen earlier, now pulling up to block the road. The driver's door opened, and a man stepped out. Tall, bearded, shaggy. Calm as he walked over and crouched beside Alice. "Where?"

Relief cracked through her voice. "Over to my car. It's the blue one."

The dog yelped as they lifted him, and Alice gritted her teeth to keep tears at bay. Blood dripped with each step it took to reach the stretch of gravel by her car.

Magdalene came back into herself enough to open the driver's door and watch them settle the dog on the ground near the trunk. A fresh cigarette hung from her mouth. "It doesn't have a chance."

Alice ignored her and knelt beside the coonhound again. Now in some safety, adrenaline cleared her mind and training took over. The man crouched nearby while she felt along the dog's spine and ribs with careful fingers. Alice glanced over at him and saw in his furrowed brow the same worry she felt. When clear, green eyes looked into her face with a silent question, she answered with a shake of her head. Even with prompt medical attention, it would be touch and go.

"Well?" That came from Magdalene again.

Before Alice could respond, whistles and shouts rang out. Three men holding rifles and wearing safety vests emerged from the trees on the other side of the road. Hunters.

Alice called to them. "Here! One of your dogs was hit by a car."

The burliest of them swore and ran over; the other two continued after the remaining dogs, voices quickly muffled when they disappeared between the trees.

After the hunter reached Alice and the dog, she said, "He's in shock. The spine feels okay but he might have broken ribs."

"You a vet?" The man had a grim, hard face beneath his beard, but his eyes were wet as the dog whined and tried to wag his tail at him.

"She never made it that far." Magdalene sounded conversational, her shades back in place as she leaned against the opened door of the car.

Embarrassment was a dim pulse in the back of Alice's mind. There was an injured animal in front of her, and it needed help. She looked up at the hunter. "She's right. I've only had some training. Your dog needs to see a vet as soon as possible. We'll take you if you don't have a car nearby."

"We're busy," said Magdalene, lifting her shades. "We're—"

"We'll take you." Alice's voice remained firm, and once Magdalene fell silent, she added, "We'll have to put the back seats down and sit with him. Can we get by without a muzzle, or is he the type to bite?"

"He's all right that way."

"Then let's move him."

It was only when the coonhound was gingerly settled in the back of the car, both Alice and the hunter squeezed in as well as they could manage, that she realized the man who had first helped her had disappeared. While the hunter gave directions to a silent, white-knuckled Magdalene, Alice glanced out the window, wondering whether the man had moved onto the family stuck in the ditch. But no, they remained huddled in their seats, the mother on her phone and the father soothing the children. A closer look around revealed the road clear and the camper van gone.

While the hunter spoke to his dog in low, soothing tones, the smell of blood and wet fur filling the car, Alice saved a bit of thought for that helpful stranger, regretting that she hadn't paused to thank him. Then there was nothing to do but keep the dog still while the black road stretched out before them.

Beasts are pure at heart. Not innocent or filled with unconditional love, or even free of malice. But there is an immediacy to their motives that humans have lost. This is why they are good enough to simply bite when angry.

Alice found that preferable over Magdalene's simmering silence while they drove out of the vet's parking lot, heavy rain pelting against the windshield. Spots of blood dappled Alice's shirt where she'd helped carry the dog in, but Magdalene didn't offer to go home, instead taking the highway on-ramp to the grocery store. Alice supposed she was to wear the stains as a mark of shame, but like many of Magdalene's points, spoken and otherwise, their symbolism was destroyed by quiet practicality. Alice zipped up her coat to cover the bloodstains before she went inside—alone, since Magdalene refused.

Two Miles was a squat, unassuming store that served every basic need, from groceries to hardware and clothing. The selection was small but enough to get by in a pinch, and Alice noticed the produce and meat looked fresher than what many of the big grocers back in the city offered.

Despite it being an afternoon bogged down by rain, she wasn't the only one in the store. A group of boys roamed the aisles, gangle-limbed and fuzz-faced enough to suggest they were in high school or just out of it. Their restlessness and greedy eyes made her nervous, and she hurried with the shopping, her focus narrowing on them until she ran into someone.

Alice gasped an apology against the slide of a wet jacket and the heat of a body beneath it. Face red with embarrassment, she looked up and saw green eyes gazing back, the dark eyebrows above them slightly raised.

"It's you," she said. The man who had helped her.

He nodded. "Did the dog make it?"

"I don't know. Things didn't look good when we left." It hurt, the probability that the dog was already dead from injury or euthanization. Alice had to turn away from it, focusing instead on the jars of honey waiting on the top shelf. She wasn't tall, and strained to reach them.

The man *was* tall, and plucked a jar for her. When their fingers brushed, she felt his calluses.

"Thank you." After she put the honey into her basket, Alice added, "Not just for this, but for keeping me from being run over on the road."

He was certainly enigmatic, offering nothing more than a shrug. But he also remained intent on her, and the silence from him felt curious instead of awkward. A burst of laughter at the other end of the aisle interrupted whatever he might have said. It came from the group of boys, who eyed them both.

A change rippled through the man for all that he didn't do more than look over. A sharpening of his gaze, rising tension in his stance. It reminded Alice of an animal on alert, taking a split second to decide whether to fight or run. Then he jerked his head at her, the signal silent but perfectly clear. *Get out of here.*

She did, glancing back to find the boys now focused on the man alone. She wasn't sure how well they'd picked their target if they planned to do more than make fun; the man was shabby like a vagrant, but there were no signs of grey in his dark beard and hair, and the shoulders beneath that battered jacket looked broad and powerful. But sticky patches on her shirt reminded her that she'd already poked her nose into a bad situation. Magdalene might swallow her tongue if Alice showed as much concern toward a man.

Her hands shook from spent adrenaline while she handed over the money and picked up the bags, but the tired-looking cashier didn't spare another glance in her direction. The boys could still be heard laughing.

When Alice stepped outside, arms already straining with the weight of a week's worth of groceries, she found two people standing at the driver's window of her car, laughing with Magdalene. Alice's heart sank. She recognized them: Rob and Darby.

Rob knew Magdalene from when they were children growing up in the same small town. Now he was a photographer who had reluctantly entrenched himself in a commercial career. It seemed to Alice that he always looked at other people with a tinge of irritation, as if unable to understand why the world at large wasn't as neatly arranged as his photographs. His wife, Darby, was a genre writer who no longer bragged about her three-book deal now that the dismal first-week sales of the second novel had come out. Both tolerated Alice, and Alice actively hated them.

Yet she pasted a smile on her face and continued to approach when Darby looked over. The other woman brushed magenta hair from her eyes, her round doll's face slack with unfeigned surprise. "Oh. Alice. Magdalene didn't say you were here."

Out of the corner of her eye, Alice saw Magdalene smirk, and resigned herself to forthcoming ugliness. "Here on a break like us?"

"No way. I'm not as lucky as Magdalene. Can't wait for inspiration to strike or my publisher will drop me."

Alice felt herself bristle for Magdalene's sake, but Magdalene only smiled and said, "They must be patient up to a point. Your last book sold thirteen copies in its first week. That's not exactly an instant return on their investment."

Rob cleared his throat, eyes nervous behind his glasses, but Magdalene wasn't finished.

"But stop worrying about such bullshit bureaucracy. There's too much artist in you. You'll crush yourself. *The Strange Life of a Clockwork Girl* is the only fantasy I've read to rise above the tepid waters of the genre."

Alice watched Rob, who relaxed again with a small smirk. He knew Magdalene's use of compliments as well as she did, that her tongue was never sweet even when it seemed so. But Darby wasn't so experienced, and offense, uncertainty, and pride fought with each other in her eyes over Magdalene's words. Even though Alice didn't know the other girl well, she picked out the exact moment Darby fell for Magdalene's strange mix of insult and praise. It was when Darby's expression took on a light that Alice had used to see reflected in the mirror.

"Bullshit," said Rob, voice lowering to a velvet purr that Alice only ever heard him use with Magdalene. "Unless you think the great Borges was an untalented hack."

"He was a dreamer. He's also dead. It's the living writers who are important now." Then Magdalene glanced at Darby, giving her a slight smile while Rob shook his head.

Alice had long grown used to falling invisible among a handful of artists primping themselves like peacocks, and only shifted her grip against the handles of the grocery bags, which had begun cutting into her fingers.

Darby shrugged, trying to act nonchalant, but her plump lips curled in pleasure. "Anyway... our house is being rewired, leaving us in the shit for two weeks. Rob's cousin is letting us crash at his vacation lodge over at Sugar Pine. You guys can always take the extra bedroom if the cabin isn't working out."

Alice demurred. "It's old but comfortable enough."

When Magdalene didn't say anything, Rob glanced at Alice. "Come on. Give us a straight answer. Want to join us for a few days or what?"

"Yes," said Magdalene.

Alice's grip tightened against the handles. "No."

The husband and wife team were both psychonauts. Alice knew from past experience that nights with them meant a round of hallucinogens and a foursome with pompous reasons for both—exploring altered states of mind to gain spiritual insight, perhaps. Or transcending the mundane world to find the beauty beyond. The usual high-concept bullshit.

"Then it's just me." Magdalene opened the driver's door and got out in a cloud of smoke. "We'll leave Alice to her groceries."

Alice's mouth went dry, and the first tremors slid through her body even while she fought to keep her expression pleasant.

Magdalene knew how she'd react, damn her, but Alice wouldn't give her the satisfaction of seeing it.

Darby had already refocused her attention on Magdalene, but Rob at least gave Alice a final chance. "You sure?"

She nodded, hoping her voice wouldn't sound strangled. "I'll be busy, anyway. I'm making apple pie."

The surprise in Magdalene's eyes was worth the horsey laugh from Darby, who never liked appearing out of the loop with inside references.

Magdalene recovered quickly. "Here."

The car keys flashed through the air toward Alice, but with her hands twined in handles, she could only note where they dropped in the slurry of mud and water.

"Thanks." This time, she couldn't keep the frost from her voice, and a significant look passed between Rob and Darby. Alice had no doubt she'd be a topic of conversation later.

Magdalene's final words to her were tossed over her shoulder. "By the way, there's a leak in the attic."

Tears burned and threatened to spill, but Alice only nodded. She knew what this was about; revenge for putting the dog over Magdalene, yes, but something subtler, too. A warning that Magdalene knew what really hurt her.

Back into the store, then. The boys were still there, and still goading the green-eyed man with overloud comments while waiting behind him as he paid. His expression was enough to send Alice shrinking back, and she caught gleams of nervousness in the boys' eyes, too. They reminded her of crows trying to puff up their courage enough to attack an owl. The cashier kept quiet, the closed look on her face suggesting she didn't care what happened as long as it wasn't inside the store.

With a searing glance in their direction, the man left with his things. Alice bit her lip when the boys trailed after him, but again reminded herself not to get into further trouble.

She grabbed anything that looked vaguely useful in the tiny hardware section. Plastic tarp, tape, rope. She left the store just as the van trundled out of the driveway with the man behind the wheel. A shout drew her focus to the opposite side of the parking lot. The three boys huddled together, two holding the third upright as he bled from the mouth and nose. So they *had* picked the wrong target.

She walked to her car quickly, furtively, shoulders hunched in an instinctive attempt to remain unnoticed. The windshield wipers beat a steady rhythm as she got on the highway and started the long drive back to the cabin.

For the rest of the day, Alice worked through domestic chores. Despite Magdalene's absence, an atmosphere of contempt lingered in the cabin like a layer of grime, and the only way Alice knew to fight it was to play the part to the hilt. She did laundry, starting with her muddied, bloodied clothes. She wiped cobwebs from the walls and dust from the shelves. Cleaned water deposits and rust from the bathroom tile. Scraped dried soap scum from the porcelain tub.

When she felt exhausted enough that her muscles trembled and weariness dulled the anger in her mind, Alice at last turned her focus toward the attic. Magdalene hadn't lied. A puddle claimed space between a drawerless dresser and a coat rack, added to every few seconds by a drop of water. Alice aimed her flashlight at the ceiling. The wooden boards looked whole and sound. She'd have to go on the roof to find the problem.

Still, Alice lingered, curious to see what space Magdalene had carved out for herself. A table waited beneath a small, round window that faced north. Dust covered the varnished wood, leaving the handprints on the legs all the more obvious. Magdalene must have muscled it out of the jumble of furniture filling all corners of the attic.

On the table, several fat candles sat in pools of their melted wax. Beside them waited the empty wine bottle from the night before, and one of the moleskine journals that Magdalene had long stopped writing in. Alice also saw dog-eared, handwritten notes held together with paperclips. She brushed them with light fingertips, easily imagining Magdalene slouched there, the little tongues of flame flickering while she fought for words that had once come so easily.

Then Alice's gaze fell upon letters scratched into the desk, fresh enough that wood dust surrounded their sharp shapes.

I N D I

"Indigo," she said, softly, and a pang went through her heart. She dealt with it by turning away to see what Magdalene had left untouched. Cardboard boxes with corners chewed open by rats were stacked around upholstered chairs worn grey by time and dust. Alice pushed aside tepid watercolor paintings of flowers, old coats piled together, and a few hat boxes, searching for anything more interesting than tired, unwanted belongings. Somewhere in the back of her mind, she wondered at the fruitlessness of going through old junk instead of repairing a bad leak, but she supposed she wanted to find a bit of color or a piece of interesting history to take back downstairs with her. Anything to keep herself from feeling so alone.

The first thing that didn't look decrepit was a trunk sealed tightly enough to keep out rats. A mixture of men's and women's clothing filled it, surprising in their well-cared for state. Modern, unlike some of the clothing left to molder in the open. Alice guessed a trunk was safer than a closet in a drafty cabin like this. Alice guessed plenty of things when it came to her maternal grandmother, whom she'd never known.

A second trunk even further back caught her eye, the dyed leather exterior a rich burgundy even through the layer of dust. Alice squeezed past a coat rack and elk-sized antlers balanced on a chair to reach it. A lock hung from the hasp that kept the lid closed, a hunk of iron pitted with rust. Alice returned to Magdalene's desk for the paperclips.

Five minutes later, hinges creaked while she lifted the trunk's lid to reveal a plush, red interior. Her gaze ran over the quilted, velvet sides before settling on what waited inside.

It was a pelt. Alice took in the coarse fur, the black nose at the end of a massive muzzle, and then the short ears. A wolf pelt.

She pulled it out of the trunk in a tangle of white fur tipped with grey and copper. It smelled like animal and tanned leather. Holes were cut where the eyes had once been, and Alice realized the pelt was both cape and mask, ready to be worn.

Gunshots cracked and echoed in the distance. Alice found herself lurching upright, clutching the pelt to her pounding heart while silence slid through the trees again. The view through the round window remained as still as a painting.

She thought of the hunters from that morning, of the coonhounds baying after the bear. It was probably how this poor beast had met its end. Her fingers loosened against the fur, and then she settled the pelt back into the trunk, disgust and fascination filling her full even once the lid had been shut and the hasp flipped back into place. Her fingerprints were the only ones to mar the dust on the trunk; Magdalene hadn't discovered the pelt. Alice couldn't say why that made her happy.

Ignorant of how to fix roof shingles, she tried plastic sheeting and half a roll of tape, hoping the shabby job would last until she hired someone more knowledgeable. By then, it was evening and the cabin breathed emptiness. Determined to push herself to exhaustion to avoid another bout of dark, sleepless hours, Alice cooked for the next day. Beef stew flavored with wine and rosemary, strong flavors needing a night to meld into a harmony. Dough for an herb and cheese bread that would rise overnight in the fridge. And lastly, that damn apple pie. She even wove a lattice top for added effect.

She lit a fire and had leftovers for dinner, sitting close to the hearth while the kindling struggled to burn. With the curtains closed and the lamps on, the pitiful flames flickering against the surrounding shadow only heightened the effect of isolation. She imagined living the rest of her days in such a way, and then felt that the food she'd swallowed might come back up.

The final, brilliant streaks of sunset glowed through the trees while Alice trudged outside for more firewood. Halfway to the woodpile, her feet froze in the mud. There, between the cabin and the first line of trees, the shape of an animal slumped in a bloody puddle. The gunshots Alice had heard earlier now echoed in her head as she moved closer.

Some kind of canid, with that sharp muzzle and those triangular ears. The muck hid the color of its fur, but the beast looked big enough to be a malamute. Its sides heaved while Alice approached, her movements careful and slow. She took in its yellow eyes and narrow chest. Its large paws.

Not a dog. A wolf. Maybe the same one she'd seen the night before. Alice stopped again. Handling a wild animal was much different than handling a pet. But the sound of the wolf's panting whines drew her forward. There was too much fur to tell how many bullets had gone in or where they were, but she knew it was likely the wolf was badly injured to have collapsed so close to a human.

She knelt on the muddy gravel, taking care to keep away from those jaws. When the wolf didn't so much as twitch, Alice pulled off her gloves to feel along its spine, trying to ignore the unnerving sense of having already done this earlier in the day. The back and right ribs felt fine, but in the final rays of light she found blood streaming from a bullet hole in the chest. The wolf wasn't just injured; it was dying.

The trees shuddered with cold winds, and clouds gathered on the horizon, dark and swollen with yet more rain. With a sigh, Alice put on her gloves again and went to get the child's sled leaning against the side of the cabin. Hopefully, the ancient wood would support the wolf's weight.

The wolf was too far gone to do more than whine and twitch while she lifted it onto the sled, her muscles straining with the effort. Still, she kept well out of the way of its muzzle, and walked backward while pulling the sled to keep the wolf in her line of sight. It was ridiculous, what she was doing. Bringing a wild animal into the cabin would make any sane person shake their head. But to just close the curtains and let it die in the wilderness alone...

Once inside and eased onto a pile of blankets near the fireplace, the wolf fell still again. Alice found an old belt but decided not to use it as a muzzle; the wolf's breath already sounded tortured. A bullet must have nicked the lungs. Washing the area around the wound with warm water and clean rags was the best she could do, and Alice settled next to the wolf in the belief that the night would be a vigil, and that in the morning she'd use the sled to drag a body back out.

Time passed in the ticking of the clock and the shallow panting from the wolf. When she offered a bowl of water, a piercing, yellow gaze glanced over it, but the wolf didn't move. Funny, she reflected, how expressive a canid could be. A wolf of this size could crush her arm with one bite, but when she looked at the shadows etched in the ridges above its eyes, she found pain and misery, not threat.

Twice, she left to collect more firewood. Each time she returned, the wolf still breathed. The room smelled like blood, wet fur, and fear, and rain had begun to drum against the cabin's roof in a dull, oppressive rhythm.

Alice found herself speaking out loud in an attempt to bring something good to this long wait. "I don't know much about wolves. Not real ones like you. But there was a book about Norse mythology that I loved as a child, and I still remember most of those legends by heart. Wolves appeared in a few of them. Everyone knows about Fenrir, but have you heard about the twin wolves that live in the sky? One chases the sun and the other the moon. Should I tell you about them?"

A wolf isn't a dog. Pats offer no comfort and neither do calm voices. But every creature dreams, and in dreams are stories.

While Alice talked about the myth, the wolf's ears slowly relaxed from their fearful angle, and its breathing fell quiet. As for Alice, her embarrassment from imagining Magdalene's reactions to every clumsy description that rolled off her tongue soon faded into a strange sort of calm. She spoke long into the night, the firelight gleaming off her hair and the wolf's fur while the shadows fell around them.

CHAPTER THREE

Bared Heart

Alice didn't remember falling asleep. Instead, she opened her eyes and saw the fireplace had gone cold and grey with ashes. Muscles stiff from hours on the floor, she pushed herself up with a wince before looking over to the wolf. Or, to where the wolf had been. Bloodied blankets lay crumpled on the floor. Alice blinked and reached out, unable to believe it. When her fingers found only fabric and air, she stumbled to her feet and opened the nearest curtains, flooding the area with watery light and the reality that she was the only living thing in the room.

Muddy tracks led away from the blankets, and fresh confusion filled her mind as she took in their shape. Not a wolf's paws. Not any type of animal's at all. They were human footprints, from someone who was—she nudged her own shoe-clad foot beside the tracks to check—notably bigger than she.

Background noise slid into her senses. The faucet from the kitchen sink was running. Alice could hear the clang of the pipes beneath the floor and the splashing of water. She grabbed a piece of firewood, holding it like a club, and inched toward the kitchen, her steps beside the footprints.

A man stood at the sink, naked and calm while he washed his face. Streaks of dried mud covered most of his skin, and matted hair hung by his ears as water dripped down his dark beard. Alice recognized him even before sharp, green eyes glanced over at her. The man in the camper van.

Her fingers twitched against the log when the man turned back to the sink, every line of his body suggesting a complete lack of shame. "So. Do the brothers ever catch the sun and the moon? You didn't say."

Alice sucked in a breath. The reference to the story she'd told the wolf and no one else, how footprints had walked away from the wolf's place by the fire...

Her gaze fell on the man's chest, muddy as the rest of him. There was a patch of clean skin just below one collarbone, and a shiny, pink scar shaped like a bullet hole.

She should deny it. Protest that she wasn't crazy enough to believe the man who had helped her was also the wolf she had watched over. From the twist of his mouth, he certainly expected her to. But Alice only stared while he straightened up and turned toward her. His eyes held the feral gleam of something wild, of an intensity that humans had lost.

Something ran through Alice while she pointed the piece of wood at him, but it wasn't fear. "If you want to kill me, let's get it over with."

"If I'd wanted to kill you, you'd have never woken up." His hand brushed the water from his scruffy jaw with a soft rasp.

Impossible to tell from that hard face and dark voice whether he spoke a lie or a truth. All Alice could do was decide and trust that decision. She blinked and took in his features. Tall and long-limbed with lean muscle. Powerful instead of wiry. But his ribs showed like he starved more often than not. She noted how his fingers shook, and the pallor of his skin against his dark hair. He had survived but that didn't make him well.

With a sigh, she let the hand with the log fall to her side. "A shower would be faster, you know. The left faucet is cold water and the right faucet is hot. There's already soap and shampoo in there."

His eyes gave away his thoughts even though his expression remained blank. Surprise and suspicion fighting with a temptation to accept.

"There are spare clothes in the attic, too. I'll bring down any that'll fit and then get you something to eat. Or do you want to leave and hunt out in that rain?" As if emphasizing her words, a gust thrashed the trees outside, pummeling the roof with water.

The man glanced out the window and then back at her. "You're handling it better than most."

"I don't have normal fears. And I'm plenty crazy in other ways, too. Take as much time as you need."

After Alice turned away and approached the fireplace to gather the dirtied blankets, she heard his quiet footsteps, and then the click of the bathroom door. Her heart thumped in her chest.

In the trunk in the attic, she found a white undershirt, a zip-up hoodie, and jeans with the denim whole but worn enough to have lost its stiffness. All looked clean and big enough to fit the wolf, and she tucked them under an arm while continuing to search. Socks, woolen and hand-knitted. Rain-resistant coat. And finally, pairs of work boots in different sizes, dusty from years of waiting unprotected in the attic. She knocked them against the floor to make sure nothing had built a nest in the toes.

The bread was baking in the oven and the stew reheating on the stove when Alice checked her phone to see if Magdalene had called. She hadn't. Alice accepted it with a twist of her mouth and moved onto the local news for Perry and the surrounding areas. A soft sound escaped her at the headline of a badly burned body found beside a camper van that had been set ablaze sometime last evening. The identity of the victim remained unknown so early into the investigation.

Alice's mind jumped to the bloody-nosed boy outside the store, and the sound of gunshots while she had explored the attic. Maybe the wolf hadn't been shot by a hunter as she'd assumed. She waited for the shower to turn off before knocking at the door, clutching at the clothes until her knuckles turned white.

The wolf opened the door wet and clean, rubbing his skin dry with a towel.

The words flew from her mouth. "Who burned your van?"

He seemed unsurprised by the question. "You saw him at the store yesterday."

"The one who teased you until you broke his nose?"

The wolf nodded. "Set it on fire with me inside and stood ready to shoot as soon as I escaped through one of the doors. He didn't expect a wolf to squeeze through a window instead."

"How'd you end up here?"

"Caught your scent and remembered how you'd handled the dog. Figured if I lasted that long, I might get lucky enough to catch your pity." Then the wolf dipped his head a little. In thanks, she realized.

She licked dry, nervous lips before asking her next question, the most important one. "You killed him."

"Yes." His steady gaze said more. *You'll have to accept it to accept me.*

For Alice, it wasn't even a conundrum. That was her great flaw, to accept all of a creature. Maybe madness was a better word for it, to take in a beast and a murderous one at that, and then to still set out a place for him at the kitchen table. To feel bewilderment tug insistently and yet fail to draw her away from a curiosity that burned like fire. Even while nerves cast her eyes down, she peered beneath her lashes at the dark trail of hair that led over an etched stomach to an uncut cock and large, heavy-looking balls that would be quite the handful. It had been a long time since she'd had a man naked before her, but she didn't flush and she didn't flinch.

Yes, it was madness, the same sort that had drawn her to Magdalene. The thrill of stepping into the dangerous unknown. And now, like then, she was too weak to resist the temptation. Alice's gaze once more met the wolf's.

"The two wolves will catch the sun and the moon during Ragnarok—the end of the world." Then she held out the clothes.

His eyes glittered; she'd surprised him again. Or perhaps he found all humans surprising. His fingers brushed hers, taking the weight of the fabric away. "When's that?"

"No one knows."

"Don't seem much like wolves to me. If you can't catch what you're chasing, you hunt something else."

"Well, it's a human story." Then Alice had to look away, because they stood too close and she'd caught the smell of clean skin and a hint of musk that even soap and a hot shower couldn't wash away. It was how all men smelled to her. Not pleasant or unpleasant, but unmistakable. Arousing.

She tried to collect her thoughts, all too aware of the wolf's gaze intent on her face. "Anyway. I set out some boots by the fireplace. Hopefully you can find a pair that fits."

The wolf nodded. "What's your name?"

"Alice."

"Thank you, Alice."

His voice turned her name into something more, and she had to breathe deep to keep her expression unflustered. "The food will be ready in a few minutes."

He ate more neatly than she expected, spoon quiet against his bowl and not a drop spilled while he sopped up the stew with a piece of bread. Alice wanted to pepper him with questions, but the set of his shoulders suggested a lingering wariness, and though there were moments when the food seemed too good for him to concentrate on anything else, his gaze always darted back to where she sat, warming her hands with the cup of coffee she'd made for herself.

When his bowl was empty, she straightened up and saw the accompanying flicker in his eyes. "Want some more?"

Their fingers touched again as she took the bowl from him, sending a tingling through her skin.

While she ladled a second helping, the wolf spoke. "You're no dyke."

It startled a laugh out of her. "What makes you say that?"

"I smell the other woman on you. But I also smell how you react to me." This time, his fingers brushed hers deliberately as she handed back the bowl. A challenge to deny what he'd said.

She deflected it with a smile. "You're right. I'm bi."

Then she sat across from him, slicing some bread for herself. "Before Magdalene, I went out with men. Boys, really, since I was just a girl. The last one was a sweet guy named Caleb. I looked him up a few years ago and found him married with two kids and on his way to becoming an assistant district attorney."

"Don't sound too beat up about it."

"I would have been a bad wife for him."

The wolf continued to eat, but his focus was split between the bowl before him and her face, and curiosity gleamed in his eyes.

Should she change the subject and talk about something dull and safe? Why trust him with feelings she'd kept locked away in her head for years? He was something that wasn't supposed to exist, a literal monster emerged from the darkness of the woods. And like any monster, he killed. But after so many years spent with Magdalene, a savage mauling no longer scared her. It was refreshing, talking with someone honest about their nature.

When she spoke, the words were hesitant only because she'd never expected to say them out loud. "Whatever is between Magdalene and me turned to shit a long time ago, but I haven't changed that much. I could never be a socialite always ready to show up at events. The publicity tours that Magdalene had once *The Chrysalis* took off only proved that. All that fake smiling and banter. I need something... not dangerous, exactly. Just something that runs deeper than what you say and wear. I can never put it into words. That's why I always admired Magdalene's gift for language."

The furrow between the wolf's eyebrows deepened while he studied her. Probably, she had confused him. She'd certainly confused herself.

"This cabin yours or hers?"

Alice relaxed at the change in subject. "Mine. It was bequeathed by my maternal grandmother. She died two years ago."

He nodded, looking as if he'd expected that response.

"You knew her," said Alice, sure of the answer as soon as she spoke the words.

"A little. Patched some of the chinking in the walls here, awhile back."

"I never met her. What was she like?"

"Curious about things."

His grimace left her smiling. She could well imagine how curiosity must have come off like nails on a chalkboard to such a terse man. "Like me?"

"No. She wasn't nice."

Memories flashed through Alice's mind. The careful avoidance of her grandmother's name. Her likeness cut out of family photos. "That might be why I was never allowed to see her."

"But you have other family? Father, mother..."

At that last word, Alice's stomach tightened. "Sort of. I send my dad and stepmom a Christmas card every year. They don't like Magdalene, so we had a polite falling out and agreed not to see each other until something changed. That was five years ago."

"Then you're alone."

"I have Magdalene."

"Who isn't here."

The words sent a flare of old panic through Alice. She set her half-eaten slice of bread aside, knowing she couldn't stomach another bite without it coming back up. "She's making a point. Once she's ready, she'll be back."

The wolf had stopped eating. Maybe because his bowl was nearly empty again, maybe because of what she'd said.

"Not for a few days, though," she added, in case he wondered at the likelihood of needing a quick escape route to avoid an ugly scene. "The lesson has to stick."

Then, embarrassed by her open neediness to be heard, Alice took a sip of coffee and changed the subject. "I don't know why I'm talking about myself. You're the mysterious one."

"Ask if you want."

The offer was made without enthusiasm, but she leapt at the chance. "What will you do without your van?"

"Wasn't really mine. I found it in the woods one day and started using it."

"Oh. How did you come to know my grandmother?"

"Found her—this—in the woods, too."

"But you didn't use her. Or this."

The wolf pushed aside his bowl and leaned forward, settling his elbows on the table. It brought their faces closer together, and again Alice had the feeling he scrutinized every visible inch of her. "No."

Despite his brief, unhelpful answers, the wolf waited for more questions with an expectant air.

"Do you have anyone who can help you? A family or a... a pack?"

The wolf shook his head.

Desperate for a firm response, Alice said, "What's your name?"

"Colton." Now he looked amused at her exasperation. "Might as well get to the questions about what I am and how I can shift between forms."

"Existential problems are beyond me. I leave that up to Magdalene. You're a man who changes into a wolf and a wolf that changes into a man. It seems straightforward enough."

When silence followed, Alice got up and brought over the apple pie, plates, and a pint of vanilla ice cream. "Any room for dessert?"

Any doubt about whether Colton had a sweet tooth was answered by the look on his face. "Two slices and three scoops."

He ate it all without a struggle and then leaned back in his chair, every line of his body suggesting satisfaction. Alice worked through hers more slowly, and by the time she finished, he was nearly asleep in the chair, stirring only when she rose from the table.

She glanced out the nearest window while taking their plates. Rain pounded against the trees and ground. "You better stay if you have nowhere else to go. At least until you're recovered. I saw you favor that shoulder a few times just while eating."

When he grimaced again, she knew it was the closest he'd come to agreeing.

There wasn't a second bedroom; the couch by the fireplace would have to do. When she apologized for that, Colton only shrugged. "It's inside."

As if that was all he'd ever ask for. Perhaps it was.

She found extra blankets for him, clean ones, and built up a slow-burning fire. The day passed in the rhythm of feeding logs to the fire and washing laundry once she found another trunk in the attic, one filled with clothes that were a bit dustier but still in good shape. Colton slept there on the couch, hardly twitching even when the fire popped and crackled.

Occasionally, Alice's glance over would turn into a long look while she wondered at the strangeness of what she'd brought into the cabin. It wasn't enough to shake her mind from thoughts of Magdalene, but it helped later, once she crawled into bed for her nightly ritual of staring at the ceiling until sleep crept over her.

In the dark, the impossible joins the possible. Humans lose their strongest sense—sight—and return to ancient fears. Unprotected under a vast sky. Helpless on impassive rock. Blind to what might be waiting. A fire offers warmth and a small circle of light, but it also instills the itching dread of being seen for miles by whatever might lurk beyond those precious few feet of illumination.

Only beasts are comfortable at night.

Alice woke to a rumbling punctuated by crackling wood. *Earthquake*, was her first thought, and she jerked up in the pitch black. But the bed didn't buck or shake while she fumbled out of it, and nothing fell until she knocked down the lamp in her attempt to find the switch. Then the noise strengthened into a roar, and animal panic pushed her outside into the driving rain, barefoot in the mud from the base instinct of trying to see where the danger was to escape from it.

Everything was blackness and water. Alice swayed, panting shallowly while the rumbling continued. The puddles that lapped at her ankles frothed with hard, unrelenting drops, but the ground beneath her soles remained still and steady. Not an earthquake, then. Something else. Something that might be racing toward her, but from which direction?

Hands caught Alice from behind and she shrieked, voice thin against the roaring. An unshaven face scraped against her neck, Colton's fingers pulling her sodden hair aside so he could shout near her ear and be heard over the hissing rain.

"It's not headed this way. Get back in the cabin."

"What is it?"

"Landslide."

"How do you know we'll be safe inside?" Alice resisted the pressure of his grip, imagining the cabin swept away with them caught and crushed between splintered wood.

"Because I know which area it is." Another tug at her arms.

"In the dark?"

She flinched from his hands when a flurry of snapping noises echoed like gunshots. Trees were being knocked down. The roaring seemed endless. Panic drove her from his grip, drove her forward into the inky black. Then Colton grabbed her again, harder than before, and the already confusing dark spun as he flung her over his shoulder. The sound that came out of her was less a gasp than a grunt of shock while he carried her away, ignoring her even when she clawed at his back.

Inside the cabin, the world spun again while he set her upright. Alice lashed out through her dizziness, slapping him across the face.

He shook it off like the rain and turned on the nearest light, revealing them both to be soaking wet and splattered with mud. "Anything that pays attention to how the ground moves knew it was coming. The hill's been weak for years and all the rain left it hardly more than slush. The part of the slope that's just collapsed will slide down in the valley, not off to the side where we are. There's no danger."

As if punctuating his words, the roar dwindled to a rumble. A few, final snapping noises cracked in the distance. Then there was only the drumming of rain.

"See?" Irritation laced the word.

Alice said nothing. Water dripped down her face. Her heart pounded until she thought her ribs might crack. Lines creased Colton's forehead while he studied her. Then he glanced down at the mud covering him and left. Alice kept still, shaking, hardly aware of the sound of water running in the bathroom.

"Everything's fine," she whispered out loud, trying to fight through how her muscles spasmed and how her heart bucked. There wasn't any air in the room. "Everything's fine."

But it wasn't. Fear clawed at her, old yet devastating in its strength. She was in the thick of something very bad, something that had left her alone.

Time passed strangely. The hands on the wall clock showed five minutes had slipped by, and then fifteen. Twenty. It all felt like mere seconds.

Finally, Alice struggled through enough of her panic to search for news, fingers slippery against her phone from sweat instead of the rain. In the dark and so soon, the news reports offered possibilities instead of facts. There apparently had been a landslide and the river might have been dammed, causing a flurry of flood warnings for many areas. The highway appeared to be blocked, cutting off Perry from the rest of the outside world. Cutting off the cabin as well.

Feeling her knees wobble, Alice sank to the floor. Her fingers mindlessly pulled up her contact list, but then she stopped, unsure of who would even respond to her begging. Another shiver wracked her body.

Colton stepped through the doorway, then, cleaner and a bit drier.

She looked up at him. "It's cut us off from everywhere else. The road..."

"How much food is left?"

"A lot." She couldn't stop shaking.

"And there's still power and running water. Not much to worry over, then."

Not true, not true. She saw how the patterns from her past had superimposed onto the present. It left her voice small but sure. "You're leaving."

"Didn't say that."

"But you are. Who would stay?"

Colton tilted his head a little. Then his gaze dropped to her muddied feet. "You should clean up. Get out of those wet clothes."

The words were practical, full of good sense. Also impossible to follow. Her fingers fumbled with the first button of her pajama top but quickly gave up.

After a short silence, Colton reached for her hands, pulling her upright with him. Neither spoke while he led her into the bathroom and washed the mud from her feet, or while he took off her sodden clothes and rubbed her dry with a towel.

When his fingers combed through her hair to untangle the snarls, she rested her head against his shoulder, exhausted by the shaking fits. "I'm sorry I hit you."

His laugh was a huff of breath. "You were scared, angry. I expected it."

"It was still wrong of me."

He remained quiet long enough that she wasn't sure he'd respond at all. "Someone abandoned you once."

It wasn't a query, but Alice still answered. "Yes. I was four years old and my mother was in the middle of a nervous breakdown. She drove us out to a deserted trail in the woods—not one like this, the trees were stumpy oaks and scrubby manzanita, and wild grass bristled everywhere. When the trail ended, she rolled the windows down a little, turned off the car, and told me she'd be right back. Then I watched her walk away, not toward where we came from, but further in. She just disappeared between the trees."

Colton held her now, soothing her with his gentle hands, his steady heartbeat, and his measured breath. If before she had slapped him away out of panic, now she clung close to him out of instinct. It was strange to her, such tenderness, and it drew the words out even when her voice faltered.

"Hikers found me two days later. I was dehydrated and hungry but otherwise okay. They never found my mother. There were weeks of search parties. It's a popular hiking area. But there's never been a trace of her. She just went off into the wilderness and was gone. They asked me what happened, if she'd said anything else to me, whether I'd heard or seen anything while in the car. All I could tell them was what I knew. That she left and I waited but she never came back."

The last word came out as a wail. Then Alice forced herself quiet. She had made it sound too simple, as if the past couldn't come up and carry her away like a riptide pulling a bewildered swimmer out to sea.

Colton's voice rumbled against her ear. "So, that's what you meant about not having normal fears."

All out of words, she nodded. Her hands continued to clutch at him when he resumed drying her hair.

When he eased her back into the bedroom, she could have paused at the dresser to find something to wear. But the world had burned away for the night, and things like habits and social customs with it. What did clothes matter when she felt as raw as a slab of meat? When Colton pulled back the covers from the bed, she only dropped the towel covering her and got in. She continued to shake against the sheets until he stripped down and slid in beside her, his head settling into the hollow of her shoulder and his arm slipping over her ribs.

The warm weight of his body anchored Alice to the bed, and when their legs tangled together, she finally closed her eyes, tears leaking down her cheeks. "Magdalene knows all this. She knows what it does to me to see someone leave. To be left alone. Even after so many years, I still... and she knows."

Long moments passed, broken only by her uneven breath.

Colton's voice rumbled against her shoulder blades. Warmed the shell of her ear. "You're not alone tonight."

After a final shudder, she nodded, and her body slowly relaxed against his.

"Sleep, Alice."
And she did.

CHAPTER FOUR

Wild Desire

Alice woke up alone, blinking at the ceiling while footsteps sounded against the roof. A turn of her head was enough to take in the wrinkled pillow beside her. Then it hadn't been a dream. The landslide had happened and so had the rest.

She ran a hand over her face, trying to understand it. She'd dated Magdalene for months before admitting what had happened with her mother. When she rolled over in bed, she could smell Colton on the sheets. An earthy scent that made her think of hips grinding together and skin slick with sweat and semen. Her perspective was changing, and the safety net of seeing him as something to feel sorry for was quickly unraveling.

When hammering replaced the footsteps, she found a robe and galoshes to put on before trudging outside. The plastic and tape she'd used on the roof were now balled up on the ground beside a ladder.

Colton looked down at her from where he crouched, boots sure despite the uneven shingles. "Fixed the leak for now. Wouldn't trust most of these to last through another winter, though."

Alice tried a smile through her bleariness. "Thanks."

That only garnered another glance her way, and she realized words likely didn't mean much to him. "Are you hungry? I can have breakfast ready in fifteen minutes."

When he nodded, she went back inside.

She made a pot of coffee before anything else and had a cup to fully wake up. By the time Colton stepped through the doorway, the ends of his hair dripping with water, she had a plate for him loaded with pancakes, scrambled eggs, and bacon. A second plate for herself, and then they were sitting together at the tiny kitchen table, lit by the morning sun unexpectedly breaking through the clouds.

There was a part of her embarrassed by what had happened the night before, and at first her gaze remained fixed on the food at the end of her fork. But curiosity soon got the better of her, and she began sneaking glances his way. He looked much better, his skin a healthy color and the lean muscles in his shoulders and arms at ease instead of shaking with fatigue. Having stripped down to his undershirt, she could see that even the scar from the bullet had faded into a faint mark.

He was certainly well enough to leave. Her fingers squeezed against the fork at the thought of the long, solitary hours waiting ahead.

Just then, he glanced up. "You're a good cook. Generous."

"Since you're used to starving in the woods, I thought you could do with a big meal or two." Then she reached for her coffee cup, hoping her hands would keep still with something to hold.

"You're nervous. Still think I'll leave you trapped here?"

She traced the cup's rim. "It's nothing against you personally. After last night, you know where that fear comes from. But... yes, I'm still a little scared."

"Well, I won't. Not if you keep feeding me like this." It was startling how much he could say with his eyes. Just a slight lift of one eyebrow revealed the humor missing from his voice.

Her lips twitched toward a smile.

"Besides, I'm not done with the roof job. There'll be water damage inside the attic."

"I'd like to help," she said, eager at the chance to do anything besides brood. And perhaps, eager to spend more time in his company.

She found it easy to work with him. While helicopters boomed overhead in slow circles around the landslide's devastation, they restacked the jumbled furniture to find puddles that needed to be mopped up and rotted wood that needed to be marked for repair. It was a tedious job, but they soon developed a rhythm for it, Colton using his strength to muscle the heavier objects while Alice stacked the smaller things and cleaned the cleared spaces.

Halfway through, he noticed the burgundy trunk with the fresh fingerprints left on its dusty exterior. "So. You found the pelt."

Alice pushed hair out of her eyes, realizing too late she'd likely left a smear of dust on her forehead. "How did you..."

"Seen it once before. Your grandmother showed me it."

"Why?"

"To see if I knew how to bring it to life." A sardonic gleam had appeared in his eyes.

Alice wondered what her reaction would be if someone showed her a human skin and asked how it worked, and decided the only surprising thing was that Colton wasn't more disgusted. "Is that how you do it? How you change form?"

"No. But witches always want things they can't have. Sometimes they learn enough tricks to get them. Your grandmother tried to use that pelt to change into a wolf through spell instead of nature."

Alice blinked. It wasn't every day a relative was accused of witchcraft. "You're saying my grandmother was a witch."

Colton nodded.

All she could think of to say was, "Well, I'm not."

At that, he actually smiled. Only a brief twitch of the lips, and barely visible through the beard, but she saw it. "I know."

It took the better part of a day to finish the attic. Dinner was the leftover stew and bread. Alice found herself as ravenous as Colton, and though the silence was comfortable, neither of them spoke until they moved onto the pie, eating it together right out of the pan.

"This entire property is a disaster," she said, an apple slice sliding off her fork while she paused to glance out the window at the rotten frame supporting the woodpile. And she hadn't missed how the porch steps groaned and buckled, or how the small shed slumped worryingly.

"Still a shelter, though."

Despite the even words, something in his voice made her look at him. "Is it hard, slipping between two worlds? Going from man to wolf and back again?"

He shrugged and had another bite before answering. "It's the same either way. Find food and shelter or you won't make it through."

"So, it boils down to basic survival."

He nodded. "Comfort's nice, though."

Working together had changed the air between them, or maybe sleeping in one bed had. Whatever the cause, she risked teasing him.

"Speaking of... your hair keeps falling in your face. And your shoulders twitch like it itches the back of your neck."

"It does."

"I could trim it for you."

He fell still, eyes widening as if she had just threatened to stab him.

When he said nothing, she prompted, "You have mats. That can't feel good."

Now the line between his eyebrows deepened. Minute changes in his expression, but still the closest Alice had seen him look uncertain.

"I worked as a hair stylist through college, so I won't do a hack job if that's what you're worried about."

"I don't like blades near my head." The words came out as a near growl.

Alice nodded, knowing not to push it.

When Colton slipped outside, she half-expected him to disappear into the forest. Instead, he chopped firewood in the remaining hours of light. And that night, while Alice waited in bed, she heard his footsteps pause at the doorway, his presence implying the question better than any words.

She pushed back the covers. "It's warmer sleeping together."

He settled against her the same as before, his larger body enfolding hers. This time, she grew aware of the hard chest and stomach against her back, of the heat of his breath at her neck. And of his cock, flaccid though it was, pressing against the base of her spine. There was a tension in the hand that had eased over her ribs, like he waited for another signal. Alice suspected that even so small a movement as leaning into his touch would send those fingers beneath the fabric of her pajamas.

She kept still, and felt disappointed about it. Even after Colton's muscles relaxed and his breathing slowed into the rhythm of sleep, she remained awake, taking in the sensation of their bodies twined together. She missed being with a man. It was a yearning she hardly dared to acknowledge, even to herself. Magdalene's tongue would cut her for months, years even, should she ever mention it. So, Alice had hidden that truth deep inside, polishing the craving like a pearl that need never be seen. Only now...

For nearly an hour, she listened to the clock ticking, Colton silent beside her while she tried ignoring the sensations stirred up by his presence. Finally, desperate to feel the weight of his hand against the hot ache between her thighs, she moved until the swell of her ass pressed into him. When he didn't react, she shifted again, rubbing against a lean stomach bristling with hair and a cock already growing hard. The only signs he gave of waking up were a soft growl and his fingers flexing against her ribs.

"What's this?" His voice sounded rougher than usual.

"An invitation." She rubbed against him again before shifting her hips, hoping to coax that hand further down.

Instead, it slid up, a callused thumb rasping over her left nipple. "I don't take orders and I'm not nice."

"Good," she said, and turned to face him.

He hadn't exaggerated, ripping the fabric from her body roughly enough that her mind flashed to images of hunters tearing into prey with every jerk of their jaws. But once she lay there naked and open to him, his touch lost that frenzy, turning slow and curious. The room was dark, pitch black, and all she could see was a shadow of a shape above her. It was what she felt that left her breath shallow with lust.

A hard body kept her legs spread apart. Strong fingers traced her throat and collar bones, slid over the contours of her ribcage and stomach. Each time she reached out to touch him in return, Colton pinned her wrists down and explored with his mouth, hot tongue always avoiding her hips and breasts even when she arched into him.

Finally, Alice groaned and let her head fall back on the mattress, twining her hands into the carved frame of the bed to keep them still. "You're stubborn as hell."

A rumble of laughter above her. "So are you."

Before she could respond, he found her nipples, drawing out her voice with sharp tugs and pinches before one hand slid down to her swollen cunt and squeezed. Alice thrashed against him, panting while he stroked her thighs, slicking them with her excitement before spreading her legs wider. When he stretched over her, all hard muscle and hot skin, she nuzzled into his neck, the mats in his hair bristling against her nose as she took in his earthy smell of iron and musk and sweat. She was sweating, too, shaking even before his teeth caught her throat to keep her still. Then the head of his cock pressed in.

Exciting, the pressure of him stretching her open. It had been so long... and a dildo felt nothing like a real cock. Alice's fingers clawed at the bed frame while he growled, beard scratching her skin, and thrust in deep. Her voice turned ragged, and her hips rocked to match his rhythm.

She needed this, the delicious friction drawing her to a primal place of no words and no thoughts. Even college escapades with boys had always included the safety barriers of condoms and being on the pill. There was nothing safe about this; she was being fucked senseless.

The power behind his thrusts jostled the bed frame against the wall. It felt like his cock would split her in half. But Alice was grinning; a wild heat had overtaken her, growing every second that his hips ground against hers. When Colton shifted, moving to suck and bite at her breasts even while he maintained that furious pace, it was all she could do to hang on. Then his breath rose into a snarl, and he bit her shoulder hard enough to bruise. She shrieked, but elation rushed through her, not terror.

Colton's body tensed against hers, and she dared to run fingers through his hair, desperate to touch him while his cock bucked inside her for long—eternal—moments. When he groaned against her neck and fell still, the weight of his entire body pressing her into the mattress, her other hand slipped around to cling at his back. They panted against each other.

Skin slick, heart pounding, she turned her face to nuzzle at his, wanting to feel what that wicked tongue would do against hers. Instead, he pulled back, pulled out, and rolled over to the other side of the bed. He didn't say a word or make a move to leave to clean himself.

Alice lay there, still gasping for breath, the sweat cooling on her skin. Her entire body felt ravaged, battered, but already she wanted more. When she looked at the dim shape of Colton's back and head settling into the mattress, she wondered if he knew just what kind of beast *she* could turn into.

He got up early the next morning, acting like nothing had happened. If it hadn't been for the dried semen on her thighs and the suck marks on her breasts and neck, she would have thought it a good possibility that she'd only dreamed the experience. After easing out of bed, the soreness of her cunt strangely satisfying, she pulled on her robe and met him in the main room. He was already fully dressed and shrugging on the heavy weather coat she'd found. When he glanced her way, she smiled. He acknowledged it with nothing more than a flicker in his eyes.

"Do you want breakfast?"

He shook his head. "Need to work on the shed. The branches resting on it will rub off the roof in a few years."

Ah. The cold shoulder. Wasn't she the one who was supposed to be filled with regret?

Through the nearest window, she watched him walk through the rain and mud, shoulders visibly tense even beneath that shapeless coat. When the whir of approaching helicopters rattled the cabin, she knew the day had begun for everyone else. Time for her to slide in step, too.

A knot tangled in her stomach while she stripped the sheets from the bed and put them in the washer. Some of it guilt for sleeping behind Magdalene's back, absurd though it was, considering what Magdalene always did with Rob and Darby. Some of it confusion about Colton's behavior. With nothing constructive to be done for either feeling, she was left with working through chores and listening to the news.

As research teams, rescue workers, and reporters crawled over the swathe of land destroyed by the landslide, Alice learned that the river, main highway, and the nearest towns had all been blocked by the 50-foot deposits of debris. It would take months to clear the road, and longer to repair it if the damage was bad. In the meantime, the Department of Transportation would work to clear the snow from an alternate route that wound around mountain peaks before dipping down the valley. Alice had tried that once and found it turned a ten-minute trip to civilization into an hour's trek. Reports warned the task could take a week or more to complete.

A week or more. The skin between Alice's eyebrows pinched at the thought, and some of the old fear slid back. It sent her checking through texts and voicemails to see if Magdalene had reached out. She hadn't. Anger hardened Alice's heart into a rock, and she set to making bread dough, one that required a lot of good, hard kneading.

Flour covered the counter and her apron when Colton stepped through the kitchen doorway, dripping from the rain and smelling like pitch from the branches he'd cut. His hand scratched where the ends of his damp hair stuck to the back of his neck. She could see how the skin had reddened there, as if he'd itched it to irritation.

Without looking at her, he sat at the kitchen table, a muscle jumping in his jaw. "Cut it."

She finished settling the dough in a greased bowl, watching him. The green in his eyes didn't darken when he was angry. They simply blazed with an intensity that withered words on the tongue.

But Alice had put up with enough shit from Magdalene. She wasn't about to let another force her into the same role. "I will if you explain why you're angry about last night."

"Never said I was."

"You don't have to say it. I can see it in your face." When his glare fell on her, she refused to look away.

"The woman you came here with."

Despite her dough-covered hands, Alice turned to completely face him. "Magdalene."

He grimaced at the name. "You think she's coming back?"

"There's no question about it. I always panic when she leaves, but she also has patterns she can't break away from. One of them is needing me."

Colton's eyes narrowed, like he didn't believe her.

Alice tried again. "That's why we're still together. She has someone who will never grow tired enough to walk away, and I have someone who will never leave me. Not as long as I give her what she wants."

"And what is that?"

Alice felt a funny little smile cross her face. "A second heart that will beat in place of her own. Those are her words, not mine. She once wrote a prose piece about it in our early days together. Just for me. I was silly enough to think it romantic instead of a life sentence."

In the silence that followed, she turned back to the sink and scrubbed her hands clean. Of course he wouldn't understand. She barely did herself. "So, why are you angry?"

"I'm getting to that." His voice still sounded abrupt, but it no longer seethed.

She nodded and gave him silence to work out the right words. It lasted while she placed the covered bowl near the lit fireplace, and then while she wiped down the counter.

It was when she reached for the back of her waist to untie the apron that he moved, the weight of his hand stilling her fingers. Despite the thick sweater she wore, the heat from his body sank down to her skin as he rumbled into her ear.

"How are you going to use last night against her?"

"I don't understand."

He undid the knot and pulled the apron away in a few jerks. Then she felt his thumb hook her sweater and slide it down past her shoulder. Even without twisting to look, she knew he'd exposed the bruises left by his bite.

"Will you tell her how you fucked a man? Let him sleep on her side of the bed?"

Shock rippled through her, and now she did turn her head toward his. "No. Of course not."

Colton's lip curled as he spoke, and his teeth flashed at her with each word. "Because of her sensitive feelings?"

"Because that's not why I did it."

Then she faced him, her sweater still shrugged down enough to expose the bruise marks. "I know how long cruelty lingers. I've lived with Magdalene for five years now, and she's a master at it. To use you as a revenge fuck would mean hurting you like I've hurt, and I won't do that. You'll just have to either believe me or not."

Colton tilted his head, the green of his eyes nearly yellow as unexpected sunlight streamed through the windows. His sneer had faded.

Alice matched his gaze with her own. "Do you still want that haircut?"

Slowly, he nodded.

She looked away, letting him win that much. "Okay. The light is best here in the kitchen. Sit down and take off your coat and shirt if you don't want hair to get caught in your collar."

When she came back with a pair of barber's scissors and a comb, she found Colton stripped to his undershirt and jeans, his boots trying not to fidget against the floor.

Alice knew his pride would never allow him to forgive her if she smiled at his anxiety, and so she kept her expression only pleasant while studying what she had to work with: thick, dark hair that was wavy where it wasn't matted. She decided that even once she clipped and evened it up, there would be enough left to keep the waviness intact.

Aware of the tension in those broad shoulders, she kept her touch brief and careful while tilting his head forward or to the side for a better angle. In clear sunlight and so close to him, details she had previously overlooked now grew vivid. A freckle on his neck. A small scar on the blunt bridge of his nose, as if it had once been broken by a blow. A streak of copper in his left iris.

Slowly, Colton relaxed, muscles no longer contracting at each snip of the scissors and each chunk of hair that brushed him on its way to the floor. When she started cleaning up the back of his head, she decided to risk a little teasing. Dangerous, she knew, since he already felt wary of her intentions. It could go very wrong.

But it could also go very right. At the next chance, she leaned forward until her breasts just brushed his shoulder blades. Her sweater was thick, but not that much so, and Colton went stock still. Alice stepped back as if it had been a casual accident, keeping silent while wiping stray hairs from his skin with a towel. The next time she did it, he started to turn his head, but she stopped him with a wordless noise of warning and a snip of the scissors.

Eventually, she set aside her tools and faced him, running fingers through his hair as if studying the results. His pupils dilated.

"Not too bad. How does it feel?" she murmured.

He only frowned, drawing her attention to his beard. Her hand followed her gaze, rasping against his jaw. "I could trim this up as well. But you probably don't like blades near your neck, either."

Too far, and she knew it even before he caught her wrists and pulled her in until their faces were inches apart. Hunger had filled his expression, but so had suspicion. "Why are you doing this?"

"You're not used to someone being nice, are you?"

His grip tightened, but she still wasn't afraid, not even when he growled out the next word. "Why?"

"Why did you stay and sleep with me the night I panicked over being left alone?"

His hands flexed. "I didn't like the smell of your fear."

"Well, I don't like knowing that you live neglected and half-starved."

He searched her face, eyes hot, but let her ease out of his grasp. "You're not afraid," he said, sounding baffled. "You're *teasing* me."

She just smiled and rasped fingers against his beard again. "I'm not saying I'd shave this off or give it a silly shape. It'll just look neat and groomed."

Surprise still furrowed his forehead, but he sat back in the chair. She took it as an assent, and once more picked up the scissors and comb. Trimming his beard took little effort; she could see where he'd tried to keep it close to his cheeks and jawline to avoid appearing like a billy goat. All that had to be done was to neaten up the results, bringing it down to bristling scruff instead of straggly, unkempt hair. From his expression, she knew better than to bring her scissors to the hair on his throat, instead letting it trail off near his Adam's apple.

"There. Not so bad, was it?"

Colton caught her wrists again, and this time, he didn't stop. Before she could say a word, his mouth was on hers. His kiss was rough, almost desperate, one hand sliding up to the back of her neck and keeping her close as if he feared losing her as soon as he let go. He growled deep in his throat when she pulled his undershirt loose and worked at his pants, but she knew it wasn't an unhappy sound.

When he started to drag her onto his lap, she resisted, trying to ease out of his grasp. "Wait."

His head tilted to the side, eyes feral. Still suspicious. She traced the bulge in his pants and glanced up with a smile, watching his expression change. As soon as he released her, she pulled his half-hard cock free and kissed the head until he shuddered. He tasted like he smelled, a primal tang that left her rubbing her thighs together. Wanting more, she moved her mouth. His sack was hairy as the rest of him, fat and heavy against her fingers. She nuzzled at it, making sure the heat of her breath reached him. His groan sent a thrill through her, and she smiled again, knowing he could feel it. Then she started to play.

There were some things that Alice knew about herself without understanding why, and the need to please others to feel pleasure was one of them. Each raspy groan she drew out of Colton pulsed throughout her, leaving her hot and swollen. Her mouth teased, sucked, toyed. Planted kisses and lathered spit. Worshipped him.

When she paused, it was only to shift her attention to the cock in her other hand, and she took a moment to admire what she saw. It looked like an ancient erotic carving, a pagan's idol. Arched and throbbing and the very image of sexual power. Alice knew from last night how the strength behind his lust could leave her limp with bliss. Now she wanted to show what she could do.

She did, taking him in deep to prove her hunger. A thrust of his hips sent his balls slapping against her chin, startling a laugh out of her, but she kept sucking, drawing him to a feverish pitch until she could see the vein that led from his hip to his cock throbbing. It was its own reward, how this terse, sullen creature writhed and swore under his breath just from her mouth.

Her jaw was just beginning to ache when he grabbed her by the head and held her still, fingers snarling in her hair while his cock pulsed. Grinning around him, she took all that he gave. But it wasn't enough. She wanted more rawness, more immediacy, even if it meant absolute filth. Once he slumped back in the chair, she pulled away from his cock to let the mouthful she hadn't swallowed spill onto those heavy balls, which had started to relax back down. Before he could stop her, she rubbed her face in the mess.

As Colton hissed at the sensation, she panted and moaned against him, the state of being sticky and disheveled bringing her close. A fumbling with her jeans and then her hand was free to slide down between her legs. She played with her swollen cunt, sore as it was, and returned to suckling at his balls, cleaning them with her tongue. His hand found the nape of her neck, his grip both tender and firm with control. That along with a final flick of her fingers pushed her to her own shuddering release, silent except for her gasps of breath.

When Alice recovered, she looked up without shame. Their eyes met. They were both slick with sweat, disheveled. Sated.

The muscles in Colton's stomach rose and fell as he panted. "Goddamn."

In response, a sound came out of her mouth, one so strange to her that she hardly recognized it. A giggle, delighted and breathless.

Colton's thumb stroked against the flushed skin on her throat, his usually sharp gaze now lazy, even amused. "Won't let you rest until you finish cleaning me up."

They shared a grin before she did just that.

CHAPTER FIVE

Living in a Dream

He left her alone for most of the day, fixing the wobbly leg on the kitchen table and then a broken hinge on the mudroom door. For her part, Alice answered phone calls and texts from people who had tried to reach Magdalene and now turned to her in frustration. Alice reassured them all through her guilt. Afterward, she tried calling Magdalene, palm damp from a sudden spike of nerves, and found she'd been blocked. Well. Not unusual. Magdalene was still making her point.

A few more concerned calls later, Alice checked Magdalene's online accounts to see if there'd been any new activity. Nothing, but Darby's bore fruit. Photos dated from the night before, done so artfully that Alice knew Rob must have been the one behind the camera. She hadn't known Darby liked bondage. She hadn't known Magdalene did, either.

"Should shake off any guilt of yours." Colton's voice rumbled in her ear.

Alice stifled a yelp of shock. She hadn't heard him come up behind her. "Do you always spy over people's shoulders?"

"You looked hurt."

"It's just needling on her part." She shut off her phone, too sick of it all to take any other calls passively directed at her, calls that Magdalene knew would reinforce her absence.

"But you'll go back to her."

Alice had to be honest, even if it meant him leaving. "Yes."

He studied her curiously, and despite the fact that his body was a man's, little seemed human about him at that moment. "She's put some sort of spell on you. Not in the way of a witch, but still a spell."

Her smile was small and bitter. "I suppose that's as good as any other explanation. A spell woven over the years."

Then she shook her head. "I need to stop thinking about it."

"I'm working on the woodpile next. The rack is rotted through."

It was his version of an offer, and she gladly took it.

The bottom logs had become soaked in mud from the incessant rain. It took the better part of a day to build a new rack on higher ground. He was a good teacher, terse yet surprisingly patient with showing her how to cut and strip sturdy branches and thin trunks to assemble the frame. By the time they finished moving the woodpile to its new shelter, the muscles in her arms and back shook with weariness. She felt satisfied to have sweated out her frustrations.

Dinner was roast duck with potatoes crisped in its fat, and then a fruit crisp laced with brandy and cinnamon. They sat together, picking tender meat from the bones by hand. When she reached for a napkin with fingers still trembling from the day's work, he caught and sucked them clean, tongue hot and sweet. In return, she later licked traces of cherry filling from his mouth. No words passed between them; no words were needed.

Later, once the dishes had been cleaned and put away and night cloaked the cabin, he approached from behind while she stared at the glowing coals in the fireplace. Without looking, she leaned back into him, taking in the strength of the muscles against her, the surety of his weight. "You're completely recovered from being shot, aren't you? Well-fed and well-rested."

His chin rasped against her temple. "Yes."

"Then there isn't anything keeping you here."

"Wouldn't say that." His hand slid between her legs, palm pressing in until the normal friction of her jeans turned into something delicious. Her shoulders relaxed, and then she faced him, already raising her head to his for a kiss.

He was deliberate with her clothes this time, undressing her just enough to leave her breasts falling out of her shirt and her underwear pulled to the side. But his touch was still rough, and Alice loved it until fingers slid down to her swollen cunt and pushed in. Pain, then, and not the exciting kind. "Wait. I'm too sore for that."

A gaze hot with hunger studied her. She couldn't tell what he thought while his fingers flexed and withdrew, and disappointment loomed when he stepped back. But then he pulled off his flannel, and next his undershirt. The firelight played over the etched muscles of his body.

"Take off your clothes," he said, voice even.

She hesitated. "Did you hear what I said?"

"Yes." He continued stripping down. "Take them off."

When she didn't move, he looked up, eyebrows rising above those intent green eyes. "Scared now?"

At that, she lifted her chin and reached for her shirt.

The floor felt cold against her bare back when he pinned her down. Unease rippled through her, snuffing out any earlier eagerness, and she scanned his face, searching for signs of what he had in mind. "I haven't been with a man in years, and Magdalene doesn't have much power in her hips. It feels like my cunt will split apart if there's so much as a finger up it."

He nodded, the heaviness of his cock and balls rubbing up her lower belly. "I'll leave you alone there. Trust me, Alice."

Thrilling, the sound of her name in his voice. Her thumb ran over that grim slash of a mouth, and when he spoke, she felt the flick of his tongue. "Keep doing that, and I'll make sure the rest of you ends up just as sore."

She traced his lower lip again before burying fingers into the hair at the back of his neck, ready to hold on. "Please do."

Then his mouth was on hers. If his hand hadn't slid behind her head, she would have cracked her skull against the floor from the force. He continued to rub his body against hers, the rhythm matching the slide of his tongue. Aching heat spread through her, and the noise she made while clutching at him sounded close to a growl itself. Then he broke off with a snarl, the rasp of his beard moving down to her breasts.

He kept his word, mauling the soft, heavy flesh with teeth before soothing with tongue. Alice's breath rose into high gasps as he teased her nipples into delicious points of agony. She thought she might tear hair from his head with her desperate grip.

Suddenly, he pulled back enough to look at her, eyes nearly black with hunger. "Hold them together."

At first, she didn't understand through the haze of lust, only aware of the slickness of spit on her skin and his erection against her thigh. When she realized what he meant, surprise jolted through her. So did a fresh wave of heat. "You *are* a beast, aren't you?"

He smiled and gave her a rumbling growl that had her hands flying to cup her breasts. Despite how the skin there burned from the scrape of his teeth, she pushed them together without mercy, watching the heat grow in his gaze over her obvious eagerness.

Colton positioned himself slowly, teasing her as she squirmed against the weight of his sack dragging up over her stomach... over her ribs... then he stretched out, hands settling somewhere beyond her head, never looking away from her face. Alice began to pant when his cock pushed between her breasts, his whole body thrusting forward at the move. Then he pulled back, their noses nearly brushing for a moment before another thrust jolted them both.

She sank into the lewdness of the act like someone sore and tired easing into a hot bath. Her fingers instinctively tightened and relaxed against her own flesh, her moans mingling with his growling while they fell into a rhythm.

The fire smoldered to nothing. Sight gone, everything she felt and heard grew magnified, nearly unbearable to her senses. The slide of his cock mixed with the scrape of his hair. How his breath caught whenever she squeezed her breasts tighter around him. The drops of sweat falling on her from him as he moved, hard, relentless. When the tension in his body increased, she lifted her head, aware of what was about to happen. His next thrust was hard, deep, leaving her able to flick her tongue against the head of his cock. He groaned at that, and then sticky heat caught her in the neck and face.

He shifted just enough to collapse his full weight against her, growling out breaths against her neck. She squirmed, not to ease the pressure but to better feel the semen and sweat between them; sore as it was, her cunt ached for the climax still building within and she needed only a little more... just a little more.

Muscles moved against her. Hands slid along her thighs and spread her legs so wide that she felt the seam of her cunt part. Her hips jerked, and jerked again when callused fingers stroked the slick, sensitive flesh that had just been exposed.

"Colton?" she gasped, now too desperate to refuse anything if it meant reaching release.

Their noses brushed before he spoke, voice still rough. "Trust me."

At her nod, his mouth locked over hers, swallowing her yelp of shock when his hips worked against hers, the weight of his balls grinding against her folds. The pressure felt exquisite, bringing her to the edge within a few panting breaths and then beyond it. She arched against the ground, voice high and pleading, nails digging into his back. He only caught her arms and pinned them still, hips now slow and hard, pushing her from a shuddering climax into a thrashing one.

When she came back into herself, she found he had rolled them both closer to the lingering heat of the fireplace. In the glow of the final embers, she caught how unguarded his face was, how relaxed his limbs felt while twined with hers. And when she traced the line of his mouth again, she felt it move into a smile. Oh yes, there was a reason for him to stay, and it thrilled her.

Beasts understand change as well as humans. They know the sway of seasons as well as any farmer, the movements of the stars as well as any astrologer. They even evoke change themselves; the beaver with its dam and the woodpecker in its hole. But many bring about change subtly, slowly. Hooves create game trails one step at a time.

For Alice, the days flowed together. News reports repeated headlines due to the slow progress, and she soon stopped paying attention other than a morning check to see if the alternate road had been cleared for traffic. The rain remained incessant, keeping her and Colton inside the cabin for long lengths of time. Even so, she never grew bored or irritated with his presence. When there weren't things to fix in the cabin, there were the mundane little chores that kept the wheel of daily life spinning.

And they fucked. Once she grew used to a man rough with his cock, she never grew tired and neither did he. When he came in from chopping wood, disheveled and sweating, she would pounce, nuzzling at the fly of his jeans while undoing his belt. And when she folded laundry, he would slip up from behind, startling her with the hot touch of his hands sliding beneath her shirt and snapping her bra open.

Quieter moments happened, too. One day, while playing with a spilled drop of coffee, she remembered the still lifes she'd used to paint with an old brush, whatever paper lay around, and a freshly-brewed pot. Nothing more than a soothing hobby formed from taking an art elective in high school. Then she had met Magdalene and Magdalene's artist friends, and had found herself intimidated among people who had broken into New York with their artwork, people who changed the definition of art itself. Yet now, in the quiet of the cabin, she found herself tempted to try again.

The first thing she painted was the coffee cup holding the very liquid she used. After that, the pots hanging by the kitchen cabinets. Then the scrubby cypresses that could be seen through the windows.

Then she painted Colton. Slyly, carefully, taking advantage of his stillness while he read or drank his own cup of coffee. The third time she used him as her subject, he dozed in rare sunshine, the light playing over his face in a way that was irresistible. She worked quietly while he slept.

Or so she thought until, unmoving, he said, "Am I hard to paint?"

She could crouch on all fours and wiggle her ass at him without an ounce of shyness, but now, caught out, she flushed. "A little. I can never get your eyes right."

He gave her one of his rare smiles. "I'm never looking at you."

And that was how he began sitting for her as if she were a true artist. At first, she'd fidget with her brush, nervous beneath his attention. But he was good at remaining still and evoking a mood with only the slightest changes in his expression, and her strokes grew more confident with each painting. For his part, he seemed to find it amusing, being the object of her undivided attention. Every time afterward, Alice would study the results and wonder if she painted him partly in an unconscious attempt to memorize every inch of his face.

In the evenings, before the night grew thick enough to draw them both to bed, he liked to read, pulling down various classics and dog-eared paperbacks from the shelves. More often than not, she would slip up to wherever he lounged and reach for the fly of his pants. Sometimes she spent hours all but worshipping him with her mouth while he read, one hand stroking her hair.

But once, Alice caught him with *The Chrysalis*, a worn copy she recognized as one of Magdalene's. She hadn't realized it had traveled with them to the cabin. The somber colors of the cover looked like a warning in his hand, and her stomach twisted while she approached.

Colton was stretched out along the length of the couch, barefoot and in nothing more than an undershirt and jeans. At ease. His glance over turned into an appraisal. "You don't like me reading this."

"It's all right. I'm just... curious. What do you think about it?"

"Not finished yet." When she made a face at him, his eyes gleamed with amusement. "And you?"

"It's too smart for me. Magdalene likes to be clever, and when she is, I can't always understand what she's saying. All I understand about *The Chrysalis* is that she's put herself into the story."

A flick of his fingers urged her closer. She straddled him, muscles tight until his free hand stroked the curve of her cheek. The teasing had left his gaze. "Does she put you in these stories, too?"

"No. When we started dating, I told her how sick it'd make me if she used my family problems for her books. I don't want those memories taken apart and sewn back together into entertainment. Writing might be her therapy, but it's not mine. Whether she took me seriously or not, it was a non-issue in the end. I'll never inspire anything of hers."

Colton raised his eyebrows. "You're very sure of that."

Alice rested her head against his chest, rubbing her cheek against the hair that bristled above the neck of his undershirt. As his heartbeat reverberated strong and steady, she closed her eyes and summoned the words for something not many people knew.

"Magdalene had a girlfriend back in high school. They lived in a small, conservative town, so it had to be kept secret. The other girl's name was Liberty, but Magdalene called her Indigo because she had deep blue eyes. I once saw a photo of her. Daisies woven into wild red hair, freckles all over her face. And those eyes. She looked like a woodland fairy. No wonder Magdalene obsessed over her."

"What happened?"

Alice wasn't the type to be fascinated by tragedy, and her next words came out in a flat tone, without an ounce of a storyteller's lilt. "While they saw each other on the side, Indigo pretended to date some clean-cut boy with a bright future. He took her to prom, but she never came back that night. The boy was drunk, and on the way home the car rolled over and landed in a ditch. Neither of them made it."

When Colton remained quiet, Alice looked up. "It devastated Magdalene. She still hasn't gotten over it."

"She's with you."

"Because Indigo's dead." Then Alice jerked her chin at the book. "Every sentence in that novel, every word, is about Indigo or the boy that took her away, even if it doesn't seem like it. Her earlier work, too."

A short silence passed before Alice spoke again. "Do you believe in ghosts?"

He only shrugged.

"Magdalene used to say that Indigo came to her. Sometimes in dreams. Or things would be moved around in her room. I always thought she wanted to see what I was gullible enough to believe, but now that I've met you, I wonder... Magdalene hasn't seen Indigo since finishing *The Chrysalis*. Maybe there's just nothing left to say about it all, but she doesn't like hearing that. To her, she's lost Indigo twice. Once in real life and once as a muse."

Colton closed the book, studying her. "And that makes up for being a complete cunt?"

Alice winced but didn't try to deny the observation. "I think it explains some things."

"Everyone's got problems."

"She can't deal with hers." Then Alice nuzzled his throat, tired of feeling bitter and wishing for something sweet instead. From Colton's huff of a laugh, he knew she tried to distract him. But he still let the book drop to catch the back of her neck, drawing her mouth up to his.

Later, he picked it up again while she remained curled against him, clothes shredded and skin sticky with drying sweat and semen. Even as he opened the book to find his place, his voice rumbled against her ear. "You're not stupid. Just got too used to her bullshit to be glamored."

Twelve days after the landslide, Alice saw the news that the mountain pass had been cleared and was now open to traffic. Her heart clenched, and clenched again an hour later when she received a text from Magdalene.

Coming back this evening.

Colton knew even before she spoke, straightening up from where he'd finished reinforcing a sagging step on the porch. She didn't realize she was crying until he took off a glove to wipe tears from her face. "It's unavoidable, Alice."

"I know." Then she tried to put on a brave face.

"I'll leave after cleaning up here." His voice remained casual, but it was now easy for her to catch the minute changes in his expression. He didn't like it any more than she did.

"What about clothes, food... is there anything you want to take along?"

At the answer in his eyes, she had to look away, well aware she'd break down bawling otherwise.

"No," he said, finally. "A wolf doesn't carry anything with it."

The sun slanted low and cold when Colton stood at the edge of the woods and stripped down to his skin. Alice collected his clothes. He told her it didn't matter, but she insisted, holding them as reverently as an altar cloth. The suddenness of it all still stunned her, and as soon as she picked up the final thing, his boots, she closed her eyes, bitter at her cowardice. The plea for him to stay, or better, for them both to go, waited there on her tongue. It died there, too.

"Pull's still too strong, hm?" Colton's voice was unexpectedly gentle.

It gave her the strength to look up. "For now. Maybe I'll leave, too, one day."

He nodded. "Have you ever worn it?"

"Worn...?"

His gaze flickered to the attic window and returned to her face.

"Oh, the pelt. No."

He tipped his head to the side, nothing more than an acknowledgment of her answer. "Never worked for the witch, you know. She didn't have the right hunger."

The cold prickled at Alice's exposed skin, and she hugged the clothes closer, aware of how little time was left. "Will I see you around?"

"In fur, maybe. No reason to stay a man."

She lunged forward, then, dropping her armful to clutch at him. Desperate for a final kiss, desperate to memorize everything about this wild, weird, wonderful creature. His mouth was hot against hers, hungry, but the bliss of scraping teeth and sweet tongue lasted only a moment. Then he stepped back, steady, calm, not shivering despite the cold air.

The change came like a flicker of shadow. One moment a man stood before her, and then there was a wolf shaking his fur smooth. Yellow eyes flashed at Alice when she gasped, and paws paused against the earth. But when she did nothing more than stare, the wolf turned and trotted away, moving into a lope as he passed the first of the firs and entered the true gloom of the woods. Silently, easily, he vanished.

Alice let out a shaky breath, brushing at her cheeks for tears that weren't there.

The cabin felt empty even as Magdalene's presence loomed once more, taking residence in corners like spiders spinning their traps. Sick in the stomach, Alice lit a fire and slowly fed it every painting of Colton. Then she cleaned everything in sight, everything he might have touched. She couldn't afford letting him linger anywhere except in her memories.

But later, when the moon rose high and full and Magdalene still hadn't returned, doubt filled her chest until it grew hard to breathe. She retrieved the pelt from the attic and sat with it cradled in her arms. For some minutes, she stared at the holes where the eyes had been and wondered how mad she was.

Mad enough to try, as it turned out. She took off her clothes, already feeling ridiculous, and wrapped the pelt around her like a blanket, fixing the head over her own until she peered out through the eyeholes. The musk of fur and animal filled her nose as she walked outside, stopping a few steps from the cabin. The stars wheeled overhead while she waited for something to happen. Nothing, except for her skin growing colder with every gust of wind.

Embarrassed, her shoulders hunched inside the pelt, and she hurried back inside. Off came the skin and on went her clothes. Even though no one had seen her, her cheeks burned at her silliness, and she folded the pelt and put it away... but not back in the attic. Instead, in her suitcase, tucked under the bed where it would stay safe.

CHAPTER SIX

Human-shaped Regret

In the morning, Magdalene returned. Magnetic, urban, gold flashing at her neck and heels sharp against the worn floor. Dark eyes burning with an inner light. Guilt bit at Alice while Magdalene kissed her enthusiastically, the taste of clove cigarettes lingering behind. A new thing, and Alice felt some of her trepidation lift, wondering what else had changed.

Magdalene draped herself in the armchair by the fireplace, eyeing the bowl of rising dough placed near the hearth. "Tried fixing up this bumfuck place, I see. Nothing else to do while I was gone?"

Alice felt the old strain settle into her, diminishing her smile into a weak twitch of her lips. "How are things with Rob and Darby?"

"If you wanted to know, you should've come with me."

"How's writing, then?"

"Mind-blowing. I've filled up half of this since last night." She pulled a moleskine journal from her coat pocket and waved it at Alice, flashing that wicked smile she remembered so well.

Alice clapped her hands together, rushing over to the chair. "That's amazing!"

Magdalene smiled again, preening like a cat when Alice ran fingers through her hair. "Are you going to read some to me tonight? Or should I read to you like we used to?"

It had been one of her favorite things to do for Magdalene in the early days of their relationship, reading chapters out loud while Magdalene listened and made adjustments in her copy of the manuscript.

"No." Magdalene tucked the journal by her side and lit up a cigarette, still smiling. "I'm doing things differently. It'll all be different. You'll see. For one thing, we're going to stay here while I work on *Vivification*—the sequel, I'm working on the actual fucking sequel."

Alice nodded, the fresh hope bubbling in her as painful as the usual fear while she watched the firelight flicker over Magdalene's dreamy face.

She went to bed before Magdalene, the sheets cold around her. The fairy tale time between her and Colton already felt faint now that the real world had once more breached the bristling forest and found the cabin. A million different worries seeped into her mind, but she couldn't bring herself to feel guilt or even shame. It was regret that pulsed in her like a growing thing, a malignant tumor feeding on her rising surety that she had made the wrong decision. Life already tried to settle around her as it once had, but the seams no longer fit neatly. Alice stared at the ceiling, fingers tangling together while the darkness pressed in all around.

She remained alone the entire night. At dawn, she rose and found Magdalene still writing in the journal, a cup of old, oily-looking coffee by her elbow.

"Are you all right? You never came to bed."

"I wasn't tired."

"But..."

Magdalene spared a glance her way, her mouth twisting a little as if finally noticing Alice. "Were you hoping for something else? No fucking while I'm in the middle of a big scene, remember? It puts more tension in the words when I don't let myself cum."

"Oh." Alice did remember, and felt a weak relief that she would have a few days for the bruises and suck marks to fade. Her skin would remain a private reminder of a cherished secret. Again, she experienced a dizzying feeling of not belonging, of no longer fitting the life she'd vacated for that brief, wonderful time.

On the third day of Magdalene's return, Alice noticed cigarette butts overflowing the coffee cans used as ashtrays. The gleam in Magdalene's eyes turned feverish, but she kept writing in her moleskine journal, sitting by a window whenever the sun was allowed to shine through the clouds.

One afternoon, Alice started to paint with her half-empty cup of coffee.

"Not me," said Magdalene, putting on her shades.

The tip of the brush wavered on the paper while Alice hesitated. "No. The wine bottle on the counter."

When Magdalene didn't respond, she kept painting. Later, while serving the lemon chicken piccata she'd made for dinner, Alice caught Magdalene looking at the results.

"What do you think?" said Alice, setting the plates on the table.

Magdalene let the piece of paper fall. "I think you should've drunk the coffee instead."

As they both sat down, Alice tried to take it in stride, searching for the brittle calm that had held her together like an exoskeleton through Magdalene's nastiest behavior. But when she remembered all the paintings burned to prevent Magdalene from seeing them, a streak of answering spite flared through her. "You hoped Indigo would come back, didn't you?"

Magdalene stared, hand frozen around her glass of wine. "What?"

"That's why you were so excited again. You saw a vision of her or something like that while drugged up at Rob and Darby's." The more Alice spoke, the surer she grew of the words. "So, when you came back here, you thought you'd brought her with you."

Magdalene pushed her plate off the table. The dish shattered, making Alice jump.

"You don't know shit. You never did." Magdalene's voice was calm, almost ethereal, but her hands had clenched into fists. Then she turned and left, footsteps fading as she disappeared up into the attic.

Alice stared at the mess on the floor, waiting for guilt to seep through her. It did, but so did something new: exasperation.

After that, Magdalene stopped talking. More days crawled past, filled with sullen silence. Sometimes Magdalene would abruptly take the car and leave for hours at a time—where, Alice didn't know and didn't ask. Instead, she responded by taking walks in the woods, her only company being a compass, a rain-resistant coat, and an umbrella long enough to serve as a walking stick over the rougher parts of the hiking trails. She could have told herself it was to get away from Magdalene's brooding, but the truth burned within. It was hope that pushed her to walk through rain, wind, and even sleet. The bare possibility of catching a glimpse of yellow eyes between the trees, of seeing one shadow out of many stepping from the thick wilderness and firming into a rangy lupine body. Or a man's.

But she never saw anything more than birds and deer tracks.

One day, she returned from one of these walks to overhear Magdalene on the phone, voice sharp and grating in a way that meant she was furious. "Just two more months. Two fucking months. God knows their editors will take twice as long to read through it and give me their shit suggestions."

Alice's breath hissed between her teeth, and her expression remained carefully blank while she walked past where Magdalene stood in front of the fireplace. Trouble with the publisher again. Things had fully collapsed to their usual state.

Magdalene hung up and stalked into the bedroom just as Alice pulled off her gloves.

"Not a fucking word out of you." Magdalene's voice shook as hard as her hands while she grabbed a pack of cigarettes.

Alice nodded and turned away, her own fingers unsteady while unbuttoning her coat. Tears filled her eyes while she stared out the window. Things would only grow worse from here; she knew it from past experience.

The instinct to survive is not always the strongest. Even in a mind worn into paths of silence and appeasement, the urge to snap and claw and kick burns like an ember hidden in the ashes. Who can say what will fan it into roaring flames, or what the fire will devour? Humans may act like beasts, too.

Paper fluttered among the ashes while Alice cleaned the fireplace, the sound of Magdalene's footsteps in the attic as steady a rhythm as her own pulse. By now, she felt as hollow-eyed and pale as Magdalene looked, and the time spent with Colton seemed as bright and impossible as a fantasy world. She was so worn down that it took her several moments to realize the shovel in her hand scraped against something tougher than pieces of charcoaled wood, and that those scraps of paper might be more than surviving bits of kindling.

The warped remains of the moleskine notebook poked out from gray ash. Alice plucked it free, recognizing Magdalene's ornate handwriting on the fire-crisped pages that had survived. Chills ran through her. Magdalene had never burned her work before.

Her fingers hesitated over the decrepit notebook and then opened it to a random page. Even though she knew Magdalene had gone up in the attic, could hear her footsteps moving back and forth, back and forth, Alice still cast a glance over her shoulder before focusing on the words held in her hand.

Her eyes have a chilling quality about them. I don't think I've seen their color before, not in eyes. It's the dark blue of deep water. Indigo. They glimmer as she tells me how long she waited in that car, holding onto her mother's promise to return.

Alice's breath hissed out between her teeth. Nothing came back in. What a strange feeling, being so angry she couldn't breathe. Like a hand had squeezed her heart to a pulp. That was how she felt—crushed. Magdalene had taken memories of her mother and used them. Not just for a story to be sold as entertainment, but to feed the image of a dead girl she'd idolized and made myth of beyond recognition.

Alice's fingers trembled as she tore out the page and put it in her pocket. Then she dumped the moleskine into the canister of collected ashes and continued cleaning the fireplace.

For the rest of the day, she gave no indication of what she had learned. But that night, after Magdalene had grown quiet up in the attic and the fire had burned down to embers, she sat on the bed for fifteen minutes, listening with her head cocked toward the ceiling for the slightest hint that Magdalene was still awake. All was silent.

The pelt looked just as she'd left it, but the fur seemed warm in Alice's grip when she pulled it free from its hiding place. Or maybe she generated the heat from the rage pulsing through her, from all the longing and despair of trapping herself when what she wanted was out there somewhere, just beyond the reach of her senses.

This time, Alice walked all the way into the woods, shoulders straight and fingers digging into her palms. The cold air bit at her bared, vulnerable body, but she didn't flinch or pause. And this time, the pelt didn't hang limp but bristled. The skin writhed against her own, and her teeth ached as the head of the pelt tightened against her own skull. Her heart pounded strangely, too fast and then too slow, but she kept moving, sinking to a crawl once she felt too dizzy to stand.

Then it was like driving through an underground tunnel, all smooth speed and darkness flickering with light, the world on the other end bright enough to scorch her eyes. Her own voice sounded distorted in her ears, thick with froth. Unleashed. What started as a scream ended in a yelp, and Wolf-Alice shook herself from muzzle to tail, paws silent against the leaf litter and damp earth.

The smells and sounds around her were sharp and strange and wonderful, and for several moments she did nothing more than sniff and listen to everything possible. The mealy stink of mushrooms. The sour pungence of a raccoon that had wandered through hours ago. The whispers of fern leaves rubbing together beneath redwoods creaking in their vast age. The forest had come alive.

She moved with hesitation at first, unsure on four paws, growing confident in letting her nose guide her away from the tar and oil of the human roads. Then she caught wind of something that spurred her into a run. She knew that scent, had smelled it countless times against her skin. Now it was magnified to her senses, potent with all his lust and power.

A cluster of cypresses to dodge around and then there was the wolf, black fur hardly more than a shadow in the mist, as if he'd known all along what she'd choose. Wolf-Alice whined and rubbed against him in a frenzy, licking at his muzzle while the tip of his tail wagged.

They ran together, disappearing into the deep heart of the woods.

Sometime in the early hour of dawn, when the pelt fell lifeless from Alice's head and shoulders, Colton changed as well. She didn't have time to do more than shiver at the chill of bare skin before his mouth caught hers, hot and fierce. Her fingers moved before she remembered what it felt like to have hands instead of paws, twining in his hair before sliding down to dig into those powerful shoulders. Dirt scraped beneath her nails. After a night of chasing each other over rolling earth and scattered streams, they were both filthy, but on him she could smell the stench of fur and piss along with the sweet pine sap and rich soil. While she'd only shrugged free of a stolen skin, he had slipped out from the life of a wolf to be with her. She shuddered at herself, shocked at her eagerness even in the face of such strangeness, but in the next moment she clawed him closer.

At her pushiness, he growled, a sound of pleasure instead of reproof. His hips moved against hers, cock rubbing against her lower belly until she reached down to grab it. But he caught her hand and broke off their kiss, a feral gleam in his eyes.

"Come back to me." It was a demand, not a plea.

She panted for breath. "Haven't I?"

When their noses brushed, she closed her eyes in anticipation of that relentless mouth, that rasp of hair. But he only teased her, deep voice a shiver against her lips. "No. You kept your heart back with her. That's why the pelt fell off under morning light."

She tilted her hips forward, rubbing against him again. "What does this have to do with hearts?"

This time his growl was short and sharp, most certainly a reproof. "Alice."

She fell still, realizing the seriousness of his words. The glow of the rising sun burnished his normally dark hair, picked out the planes of his face. The sight was too painful with what waited on her tongue, and she looked away. "If I leave her, she'll have no one else."

He growled again and crouched, pulling her hips toward his face. The abrupt move cost Alice her balance, and she grabbed onto his shoulders, breath catching when he nuzzled between her thighs.

Then he said, "She hasn't even touched you. I'd smell it."

He sounded angrier, but when Alice ran a hand up through his thick hair, he pulled her closer, tongue sliding into her slick cunt. Her back arched. She'd seen him catch a rabbit and rip it open with teeth that snapped its vertebrae like matchsticks, but it wasn't panic or revulsion that seared through her as that dangerous mouth explored what it could.

"You're right," she gasped. "She hasn't."

Then she squirmed, trying to get away from that sweet torment. They were too close to the cabin; she might be heard if she started crying out. But Colton only held on, tightening his grip until she was sure he'd leave bruises, and soon her struggling turned into her hips rocking to the rhythm of his tongue.

She did cry out in the end, a thin wail that echoed off the surrounding trees. Colton caught her when she collapsed, pushing her onto her back until she panted up at a sky just glimmering with blue. When he stretched over her, the hair on his chest and stomach scratching her over-sensitive skin, she kissed him with all the desperation she couldn't put into words.

His first thrust inside jolted her entire body; he was angry, ready to ruin her. She couldn't think of anything better, and grabbed onto the arms braced on either side of her, holding on while his savage movements continued. She answered each of his growls with a moan, digging in her fingers to urge him on. Hips slapping together, sweat muddying the dirt on their bodies... she felt less human than when she'd been on all fours as a wolf.

They fucked so hard that she sucked froth off his cock afterward, damp hair clinging to her face and nipples sore from his teeth.

"Tonight," she said, resting her cheek against him while her pulse slowed. "I'll come back tonight."

She did, and the nights after that, too, even while days remained strained with silence and the occasional appearance of Magdalene, gaunt as a scarecrow and haunted in the face. Alice learned to catnap throughout the day to be ready for those dark hours beneath the stars, when she hunted, played, and raced as a wolf. It was during twilight that she would find herself braced against a tree or the ground, panting as Colton's teeth held onto her neck. Pushing away from the heat of his skin and mouth grew harder each time, and when she returned to the cabin from a direction unseen by the attic window and took a shower to scrub the mud, semen, and blood from her skin, the spike of guilt always felt a little fainter.

She knew it couldn't go on forever but wasn't about to give up her taste of freedom. She had changed that much even without the pelt's help. And perhaps one day, the pelt wouldn't come off at all.

CHAPTER SEVEN

Punishment

"Larry dropped me, the fucker." Magdalene's voice sounded flat, unemotional.

Alice looked up from the honey she spread on the toast. "Your agent?"

"Do I know anyone else named Larry?"

Alice shook her head and brought over the plate. "I'm sorry."

"Are you? You don't look it." Magdalene gave her an odd little smile. The smell of wine hung thick around her. "In fact, you look fucking fantastic. Healthy, glowing skin, glossy hair. Tits nice and perky."

"I really am sorry." And she was.

Magdalene shrugged. "Whatever. It's time to leave this shithole. It did nothing for me."

Alice's heart froze. "Leave?"

"What's wrong? Like it here?" Magdalene was staring at her.

"I guess I do. And what about your writing? You said—"

"Who cares what I said? It's time to go. At least you can get some decent fucking food in the city."

Alice decided it was better not to argue while she was in such a state. "I'll pack the bags after breakfast."

And she did, hands trembling and mind whirling. She had to tell Colton somehow. She couldn't just leave. Wouldn't just leave. How much of a fit would Magdalene throw if she said she wanted to stay behind? Had she changed this much? Could she walk away at last?

"Magdalene?" she called, looking up at the ceiling where Magdalene's heels sounded in the attic.

Nothing except for the continued footsteps. Alice tried a few more times. Silence fell in response. What was she doing up there? Deliberately ignoring her? Tracing where she'd carved Indigo's name into the table?

Exasperated, Alice stopped packing to go up to the attic herself. She called out yet again while still in the dim stairway, trying to keep the words pleasant. "Magdalene, I need to talk to you."

But she wasn't in the attic. Alice stepped inside just to be sure, squinting in the poorly-lit room. Then she blinked, recognizing the objects left on the floor as Magdalene's boots.

"What..." She stooped to pick them up and then saw a crumpled receipt by one of the toes. Stepping close to the window for light, she smoothed it out. It was a day's fee for the local shooting range. She started shaking just as the floorboards behind her creaked.

Magdalene stood in the doorway in her socks, that odd smile back on her face. "You're not a good liar, Alice. You never were."

Then she stepped back. In a flash, Alice knew what would happen and lunged for the door. "No!"

Too late. It slammed between them, the lock sliding into place with a metallic clang. Alice's fists beat against the wood, and when that did nothing, she started screaming. Below, the front door below opened and closed. She rushed to the window and saw Magdalene walking off into the woods, her sleek woolen coat at odds with the rifle in her hand.

Alice broke everything in an attempt to get free. But the window was too small to squeeze through, and the door too well-made. Her throat grew raw. Her fingers bled from where she bit them in a frenzied panic. Finally, when the sun hung low in the sky, gunshots cracked in the distance. Alice sank to the floor and cried.

Later, the crackling of a lit fire roused her. She glanced out the window and saw it was night. Somehow, she'd fallen asleep despite the raw agony in her chest and the stinging of bloodied knuckles and an arm cut by shattered glass. The sound of the lock sliding back was a quiet scrape of metal, nothing more. Alice tried to jump up, but her limbs ached and trembled, and by the time she staggered to the door, the stairway was empty.

She clung to the handrail like an old woman, crippled by her fear of what she was about to see.

Magdalene crouched before the hearth, feeding a fire that burned so brightly her face glowed with reflected light. It was another funny little smile that Magdalene gave her, and Alice's heart shrank into a knot the moment she saw it.

"I didn't think you'd ever do it." Then Magdalene held up the pelt.

Alice said nothing. She felt frozen.

Magdalene stroked the fur, watching her face. "I saw you with him. Sat on the roof with a good pair of binoculars. I thought it was just a case of fucking some redneck in the woods. Or maybe someone from your past. Whatever he was, you looked like a nymph. Flushed and in your element. I hadn't seen that look on your face for years."

Alice's stomach roiled as Magdalene's expression changed, the stub of a cigarette trembling between her fingers. "You fucking bitch. You knew. You *knew* what it'd do to me to see you with a man. To think that he might fuck off with you."

Alice found her voice at last, although it was a small, pitiful thing. "Because of what happened with Indigo."

"Don't you dare. Don't you dare say her fucking name."

"Why not? It's always between us." Now her words shook, but not with fear. "I saw what you burned in the fireplace. You're still trying to bring her back. You have been since you finished *The Chrysalis*."

Magdalene bit down on whatever she had been about to say, and some of the slyness faded from her eyes. After lighting a fresh cigarette, she abruptly said, "I saw you change."

Alice sucked in a breath, fingers itching to rip the pelt away. But Magdalene clutched it so tightly her knuckles had gone white, and Alice was afraid of hurting it.

Magdalene flicked ash onto fur, drawing a wince out of her. "Well?"

"What do you want me to say?" Alice couldn't take her eyes off the pelt.

"Nothing in particular. Just curious of your reaction. You have a little bit of gold in your fur, but he's black as coal, isn't he?"

Somehow, hearing that was worse than having seen that page in the burned notebook. It took the time she had shared with Colton and turned it into one of Magdalene's neat descriptions. How long before she wrote a story about it? Feeling sick, Alice had to turn away.

"Alice the wolf's wife. Not 'mate,' you're a little too dull for that. But I'm sure you clothed and fed him while he was here. Didn't you? All these new fixes to the cabin—did you think I didn't notice? I'm a writer, details are the first thing I see. Whenever you try to hammer something, you hit your thumb instead of the nail."

"Stop it." Alice squeezed her hands into fists to keep them from darting up to her ears in a childish attempt to block out Magdalene's words.

"Just one more question, then."

"What?"

"Look at me while I ask it. I think I deserve that much after you cheated on me with a lice-infested animal."

Alice's lip trembled from repressed tears, and she bit down on it while turning to face the woman she had once adored.

Something like wonder filled Magdalene's face. "What's it like, becoming something else?"

"Try it and see." Alice's voice cracked.

Magdalene stroke the brindled fur again, her gaze dropping to the pointed muzzle, to the eye holes cut into the face. "No. I think some things are best left a mystery."

Then she flung the pelt onto the fire.

Alice screamed as if it were her own skin being burned. Magdalene's eyes shone brightly while flames rushed over the pelt, and when Alice lunged for the fireplace, she held her back, arms flexing with a wiry strength that would leave bruises.

As the smells of blood and burning hair filled the room, Alice sank to the floor, still in Magdalene's arms. The cries that came out of her mouth were harsh, ugly things. Snot ran down her face while she thrashed, still reaching for the ruined thing in the fire, but Magdalene pulled her close until their cheeks rested together.

"You would've left me. I need you, poor Alice."

Alice only stared as the blackened mass that had been the pelt twitched and contracted from the force of the heat and flame eating it away. As soon as Magdalene's grip eased, she broke free, stumbling back from the fire. Her words came out thick and flat. "You just lost me for good."

She didn't remember running, but there she was in the bedroom, slamming the door behind her and pulling a chair in front of it. Magdalene knocked, then pounded, and then finally yelled while Alice finished stuffing her suitcase with whatever she could grab. The cabin was hers, but she couldn't stay in it another day, not even another minute. Not with the smell of burned hair choking the air.

Silence fell only until Magdalene appeared outside the window. "Alice. I hate hysterics."

Alice grabbed a bronze statue of a huntsman and threw it at the window. Magdalene ducked away in time and stared through the broken glass. Something new entered her expression. Fear.

Alice resumed packing. "You finally took too much from me, you cold, callous cunt. Now you won't be getting anything else. Not my love, not my time, and not my attention. I pity the next girl who falls for you without realizing you're just too empty to live alone."

"Are you finished?" The sneer to the words wasn't as strong as usual, and Magdalene's velvet voice sounded rubbed raw.

Alice snapped the suitcase shut and looked at her. "Completely."

Outside, she dragged her luggage behind her through the mud. Something in her expression kept Magdalene from touching her, and she headed for the car even when Magdalene disappeared inside the cabin. Frantic footsteps and crashing objects drifted out to Alice while she threw the suitcase into the backseat and walked over to the driver's door.

She opened it just as Magdalene reappeared in the doorway with a gun to her head. "I'll have to, if you leave. I'm nothing. I'm shit. You're the only thing that keeps me going. Everything else is gone. Even words."

When Alice didn't respond, her voice turned desperate. "Think I won't do it?"

Alice slid into the driver's seat. "I think it doesn't matter. The Magdalene I knew has been a ghost for years."

Magdalene started at that, and the nozzle of the gun swiveled from her head to Alice's. "I shot him. Your wolf. There's no one to run to."

One final blow, that, and it hurt as much as seeing the pelt burn. Face still puffy and raw from tears, Alice glared into Magdalene's eyes, the color of amber in the slanted winter sun. Then she slammed the car into reverse and roared out of the driveway, leaving Magdalene on the porch, gun lowering to her side.

CHAPTER EIGHT

An Ugly End

He smelled the woman on the wind long before hearing her thrash through the trees and undergrowth. Smelled the oiled metal of a gun, too, and slipped away for dense cover. No real hunter, her; she shot at him even without a clear line of sight, and none of the bullets came close.

There was some human in him, even when he wore fur, and so the wolf fought his instincts to leave the area. He knew the woman's smell, had replaced it with his own on Alice. If this cunt was after him, what had she done to Alice?

When it was safe, he tracked her scent to where it had been left on the ground and rubbed against branches. Rage, panic. Burned hair and lingering smoke. And blood. Alice's blood.

The black wolf could cover ten miles in twenty minutes on a desperate hunt, but the cabin wasn't so far, and he arrived at the porch at a dead run without panting for breath. More blood in the empty driveway, and now he found Alice's scent, thick with grief and fury.

Doorknobs needed hands to turn them, and so he changed form, walking naked through the rooms. His nose still worked better than a plain human's, and he followed Alice's trail backwards, taking in the broken window in the bedroom, the dresser drawers ripped open and empty of clothes.

At the fireplace, he crouched and took in the stench of the smoldering pelt. There were scratches on the wood floor near the hearth. He recognized the shapes, having seen them often enough on his shoulders and back, and traced them with his own fingers. Alice must've been held there while the pelt burned.

Then he found where she'd cut herself in the attic, saw the upturned furniture and battered door. Smelled Alice's scent in the room. Locked inside...

All of this was taken in with the silent patience of tracking hoofprints through the woods, but already his teeth ached to savage, and he left the cabin a wolf again. The woman's blundering track led to the river's edge, and there he found her dropping stones into her pockets with shaking hands. A gun waited on the ground, nearly invisible in its bed of leaf litter.

There was some human in him, even in this form, and so instead of ambushing her, the wolf stepped between the woman and the gun, trapping her at the riverbank. At his growl, she turned toward him, revealing a pinched face with red, swollen eyes.

"So, I missed you."

The wolf snarled, showing her all his teeth.

The woman flinched, but her eyes remained venomous. "Piece of shit. You took her from me. Are you going to take away how I die, too?"

The wolf dodged the first rock thrown at him, and the second. Then he lunged forward and was on her, teeth biting down through the scarf until he tasted blood.

CHAPTER NINE

The Anguish of Escape

Alice had checked into the first bed and breakfast she found, paying for a night's board. For several hours, she did nothing in her room except sleep, wake up to cry, and fall back asleep.

Finally, at five o'clock in the evening, she got up and showered. Shaved her legs and trimmed her nails. Braided and pinned her hair into a neat bun and plucked stray hairs from her eyebrows. Soothing little rituals of self-care that couldn't touch the massive fractures in her life. She was lost but could at least look like she knew who she was. When she dressed, she paused before putting on her bra, instead running fingers over the suck marks still on her breasts.

A knock came at the door while she shrugged on her sweater.

"Yes?"

"Alice Corrigan?"

"Yes."

"I'm Jake Danvers, the local sheriff. Ma'am, may I talk with you for a minute?"

Dear God, she went ahead and did it, thought Alice, and kept her voice flat against the numbness rising behind her ribs. "Just a minute."

The sheriff was a tall man, burly enough that his paunch only added to his formidability. His eyes gave away nothing of what he was about to say. He was cordial when she invited him into the room, but his gaze took in her appearance with the keenness of a hawk. Alice was glad she couldn't feel anything, as otherwise she'd be trembling in fear.

He wasted no time. "We found a body in the woods about two miles from a cabin listed with you as the owner. The driver's license on the body belongs to a Magdalene Bishop. Do you know this woman?"

Alice nodded. "We were staying at the cabin, but I left this morning after we got into an argument."

"Mm-hm." The sheriff didn't sound surprised.

"What... what happened?"

"A man walking his dog found the body at the south bank of the river. There were stones in the pockets of the coat."

When the sheriff said nothing else, she tried to form coherent words. "So, you're saying it was suicide?"

"No, ma'am, there's good evidence that Ms. Bishop did not take her own life."

She stared at him, fear joining the bewilderment roiling in her stomach. Magdalene was creative enough to make a suicide look like murder.

Before she could respond, he added, "Did she have a dog?"

Alice could only shake her head. "No. Why..."

The sheriff's face was lined with years, and now those lines furrowed a little more. "It looks like an animal attacked her before she could jump into the river."

The words felt like a punch, and Alice folded over in her seat as if they had been one. She felt the sheriff's hand on her shoulder, but whatever he said only buzzed at the edge of her consciousness. Further detail was unnecessary, anyway; she knew it had been Colton. He was alive, and Magdalene was dead.

When she could breathe again, she straightened up and tried listening to the sheriff.

"We need someone to positively identify the body."

Dizziness rushed through her again, but Alice knew it was the last thing she'd ever do for Magdalene. She held that thought like a flashlight in the dark while the sheriff took her to his car, lights off on the drive to the morgue. It was a cold room, but it wasn't the chill that sent prickles along her skin when she stood there and saw what was left of Magdalene. Colton had not been kind.

She threw up. Not there in the morgue, but later, while giving the sheriff the phone number of Magdalene's parents so he could notify the next of kin. Time passed in fits and starts, and her hand sweated against the plastic cup of water the sheriff had offered her. News of the strange death of a prestigious author would already be lighting up the circles back home, she knew. Reporters would come. Friends would question. She tried to examine how she felt about it all and found, strangely, a sense of overwhelming relief.

It's over.

The thought rang through her mind like a tolling bell, clear and sweet and painful in its strength.

They took her back to the motel, but she didn't want to stay, instead intent on returning to the cabin. Colton was alive, and she needed to find him. Find him and... say what? She wasn't sure, not with how her heart felt both bewildered and inflamed. As she got into her car, the sky above looked immense, as if it, too, had been opened up to her.

She stopped at the drive thru next door, the only thing open at two in the morning, and ordered a large soda, hoping the twin hits of sugar and caffeine would keep her awake through the hours.

Before she could pull out into the street, a figure in a battered winter coat crossed the parking lot to wait by the driveway, shapeless and faceless. Something about the way it stood so still convinced Alice to stop and unlock the doors. Her heart pounded while the figure slipped into the front passenger seat, easily, casually, as if waiting for her all along. A gust of wind and rain entered the car with it, and then the slam of the door separated them from the rest of the world.

Once Alice steered the car onto the road, the figure pushed back its hood. Her hands jerked on the wheel as Colton shook his head to shed the rain drops that had slipped past the protection of the coat, remaining silent. Then she saw a deserted place to pull off to the side and took it, turning off the engine to leave them in a gloom broken only by the flashing of a distant road sign.

When she looked over, Colton met her gaze with a slight lift of his eyebrows and then glanced ahead.

"You're leaving," he said, his voice its usual dark monotone.

Her response was to tug his wrists free of his coat pockets, heart pounding in her throat when two warm hands clasped her own. Violent anguish eased as she kissed those rough fingers. "You're alive. She said she..."

Then Alice shook her head, feeling herself break all over again. "It doesn't matter. The pelt was destroyed. Magdalene threw it into the fire."

"I saw it."

She lifted her face from his hands only to feel his thumbs wipe away the tears running down her raw cheeks. "Then you were at the cabin. And you were the one who killed her."

He shrugged, touch tender despite his brusque tone. "Want an apology?"

The yellow flashes of light turned his eyes into something wilder than usual, if that was possible. His clothes were scruffy, ill-fitting on his long, lean frame, and his beard already appeared shaggier, rasping against her fingers when she brushed his chin. He didn't move, but something in his gaze flickered when her thumb slid over his lips.

"She wanted to trap you." His hot tongue flicked against her fingertips.

Alice felt her shoulders sag, and she leaned forward to rest her forehead against his, hand pushing at the worn plaid shirt beneath his coat until it found the hot skin of his chest. "Didn't she? The pelt is gone."

And so you will be, too. Those were the words she couldn't bring herself to say.

Colton shifted against her. "So you can't live among wolves. I can live among men."

Impossible to keep the hope out of her voice. "For how long?"

"Until we tire of each other."

She took a deep breath, remembering how Magdalene had sworn to hold her love like a second heart. Remembering what it had turned into. Then she looked into his eyes again, finding flashes of the nights where they had run together, moonlight on fur and breath steaming. Flashes of the firelit hours spent with him rising above her huge and powerful, kissing her like she was nothing he'd ever tasted before. He was offering her his company without asking for her freedom.

"I'd like that," she said, and meant it. Then she leaned in to kiss him, unafraid even with the memories of what she'd seen in the morgue fresh in her mind.

To take a beast as a lover means to accept teeth along with tongue, and delight in both.

When Alice pulled out onto the road, Colton's hand settled on her thigh, both comfort and a promise of what was to come. Even though her eyes felt puffy and sore from tears, and doubtless would again, Alice found herself smiling. Her heart was now her own.

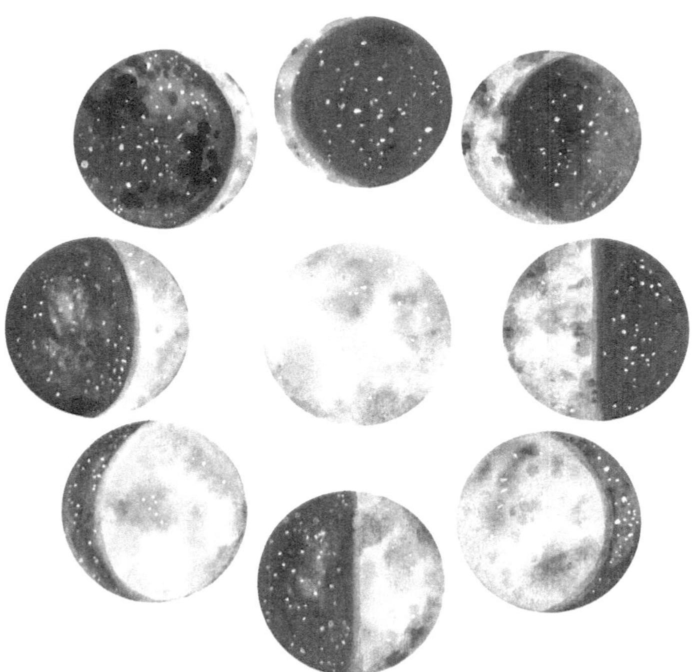

The Starving Times
A Short Prequel

The witch was hungry. She was *always* hungry. The bones in the iron pot over the fire had long had their marrow picked out with a fork; now she boiled them to draw out enough gelatin to thicken the water into broth.

Ah, how she had suffered since Ruth had left. Such a selfish child, leaving her own mother to starve in the woods like a beast. Time was, she herself could have drawn in travelers through her swaying hips and sweet laughter, or tied her hair back with a handkerchief and put on worn clothing to invoke a sense of honest toil, of clearing out a safe patch of earth in a land where trees bewildered any sense of direction and foxes waited to feed on bodies lost to the rest of the world.

But now the witch was old, and only invoked the dryness of dust on forgotten objects and the yellowed teeth of a skull's grin. When people came to her little cabin in the woods, it was by accident, and it happened less and less. She had been lucky to catch that architect.

With a sigh, she stirred at the pot again to see if the liquid inside had thickened at all. The dull clacking of the bones against her spoon consumed her senses. When one starved, one's focus always narrowed in scope to what could be eaten. And yet, even as she bent closer to the sad attempt at soup, something else brushed against the witch's shriveled mind. A taste to the air, a haze to the sunlight. Like smoke traveling from a distant fire, intangible even as it overwhelmed.

Someone was approaching the cabin.

The witch forgot the way her stomach pinched and her hands trembled, forgot the broth bubbling in the pot. She hobbled to the kitchen table as fast as possible, waving a hand over the leftover rat skulls and snail shells that rolled along the worn wood.

In the old days, when she'd been at full strength, a veritable feast would have appeared. Freshly-baked rolls twisted into fanciful shapes and nestled together in gingham cloth. A roast glistening with its own succulent fat, a proud centerpiece among the wild greens roasted with garlic and the split figs drizzled with honey. Hand-picked food, plucked from the earth and skinned of its hide.

But now—oh, how sad it all appeared. A bowl of broth with some withered carrots floating in it. Dried strips of meat as gnarled as her own hands. A wrinkled apple, its sallow color warning all of its sour nature. For the best that the witch could do in her weak state was to inspire pity instead of hunger. Pity wasn't nearly as delicious, but to a desperate stomach, even mere gruel would do.

The witch sat there with her ancient face and ragged clothes, waiting for her visitor to arrive.

The footsteps climbing her porch sounded sure and strong, and the witch's jowls nearly slavered. This would be a good meal. This would be one she could make last for the whole winter. When a knock sounded on the door, it was all she could do to sound surprised instead of ravenous.

"Whoever it is, come in. The door's unlocked and these old bones don't want to leave the fireside."

She hunched there by the weak flames, letting the creak of hinges fall silent before turning to look. Her painful movements were not exaggerated; in her state of starvation, age made itself known in the very creak of her bones, in the flabby sway of skin and the trembling of desiccated muscle. She was an ugly old thing, a vulture of a figure, and it sharpened her hunger all the more as her gaze fell upon the figure standing just inside the doorway, not yet within the reach of the firelight.

It was a man, that much was clear. One tall and broad in the shoulder. Despite the way he remained in shadow, with only the bare shape of him rimmed in sunlight, she sensed that he was strong beneath the worn clothing, his muscles well-used. Well, that was all right. She knew plenty of kitchen tricks to soften tough meat. The witch wished she could see his face—a man's face said a lot about his nature—but already she felt a twitching between her ribs. Not the savage stabbing that had happened after Ruth had left. Something much quieter but equally persistent.

Greed can rouse a heart as much as love. With some hearts, they might even be one and the same.

Did the witch love her victims in her own strange way? Was sucking the marrow from their bones any sweeter for her than for a gourmand with his dish of veal shanks? Perhaps she herself did not even know. Perhaps the answers did not even matter, not while she held out her arms toward her intended meal as if ready to embrace him. As if ready to ensnare him.

"Come in, come in. Warm yourself by the fire. My home is always open to strangers."

Some people would fumble for explanations about their presence. Some would simply ask for what they needed, such as directions out of the woods, or a place to stay for the night. Some would even bring their own form of violence and hunger, faces alight at the idea of robbing and murdering a helpless old woman.

And yet this man only stepped closer with the cautious movements of a beast. The dancing flames picked out his unshaven jaw and the mats in his hair, but he smelled clean enough. Like river water and rich earth and that particular iron tang that warned of blood.

The witch's eagerness further brightened. Perhaps the man was wounded. She hoped so; it would make killing him all the easier. "What's your name?"

"Most would ask why I'm in their home." His voice sounded deep and low, with a roughness to each word that suggested a reluctance to talk at all.

"I'll get to that soon enough. Don't be shy," she said, when he stopped just out of reach of the golden circle cast by the flickering flames. "Sit in the chair there and warm yourself. I saw frost on the branches outside the window this morning."

"The cold doesn't bother me anymore than it bothers you." Then at last the man sat across from her, revealing himself in full. His eyes said more than his face, sharp and feral as they took in everything about her. When his head tilted at the right angle, their green caught the firelight and glowed like an animal's.

It was then that the witch realized her folly. With a sigh, she let the kindly smile drop from her face, let her mouth shrink back into its normal bitter line. "Ah, I'm getting old. I thought you were human."

He watched her without looking away, and for the first time in ages, the witch felt the fear of being in the presence of something more dangerous than she. There were many things that crept through the world unknown to humans, creatures that hid in the shadows or came out only at night. Creatures that could only be pinned down by myth and legend and lore. This one was rare, a hunter that took the shape of a black wolf most hours. She'd heard they could look human enough, these beasts, when they wished to. When they grew... curious.

"What do you want?" she said, voice harsh as a crow's call. "I'm hardly good game. There's nothing to me besides skin and bone."

"I know that." He looked around with care, absorbing everything there was to see. "I'm new to these woods. Wanted to see what else was in them."

"Sizing up the competition, then?"

The wolf hiding as a man looked at her once more, and what she saw in his face made her cringe back in her seat. The firelight flickered as he said, "You're nothing close to that."

"Your kind always holds such arrogance," she muttered, too tired to remain cautious. She was cold, needled by her earlier mistake, and worst of all, still hungry. "As if you have no weak spots of your own."

"Do we?"

"That's obvious even to a half-senile thing like me. Not fully beast, not fully human. Always nosing around sweet-faced women who might like the feel of your teeth before they realize they're bleeding. You're lonely."

Something flickered in the wolf's eyes, then, but his voice remained unchanged. "So are you. Don't often find a witch by herself."

"I have a daughter somewhere, but the wretch ran off without so much as a goodbye. She's young enough to think she can leave it all behind and live among humans. I call out to her, sometimes, but she never answers. Not yet, anyway."

When the wolf only studied her, unmoved, the witch stopped trying to make her mouth tremble and instead huffed. "How long will you stay in this area?"

"Until I grow tired of it." Then the wolf stood, the shadows flickering around him.

"That'll be soon enough. I've never known one of your kind to linger more than a few moons."

But when the wolf only glanced around, looking thoughtful, the witch felt the first breath of danger stir her withered senses. Whatever he planned, she wouldn't like it. As he turned to leave, she called out to him. "There's no game to be found here. Look at me, you surly lump. I'm barely more than a skeleton."

But the wolf didn't glance back, didn't even pause as he walked out and shut the door behind him, leaving the witch to a struggling fire and a table littered with pitiful remains. She scowled at the iron pot with its bellyful of bones. That creature would keep troubling her until he had what he wished. She was sure of it.

Her instincts were worn yet true. Although she didn't see the black wolf for the next few days, she sensed him lingering near the cabin, one shadow among many in the woods.

"What are you after, you damn thing?" she muttered on occasion, withered hands still strong as she chopped wood for the fire. Even with such apprehension needling at her, she made sure to keep everything ready for a grand meal. There would be a visitor to the cabin at some point or another. There always was. And then there would be a feast, and she would blessedly feel full and whole, if only during that final bite of meat stripped from the carcass. All she had to do was wait...

And then one crisp winter morning, when the redwoods stood dusted with snow, someone came. A girl with long, dark hair and a heart-shaped face. A girl in trouble, her small tent crushed beneath the weight of the past night's snow and her old car caught in ice and mud.

"I'll freeze to death out there," she said, her coat as limp and bedraggled as wet feathers.

The witch smiled. "Then come in and settle yourself by the fire."

Oh, it was hard not to take a log to the girl's head as soon as she sat, the flames casting their glow over skin flushing pink from the sudden warmth. It was hard to give her a mug of chamomile tea instead of something stronger, something with juniper berries or cinnamon so that her very flesh would be infused with the flavor.

"Now, then," said the witch, sitting in her own chair. "My name's Franny Harford."

"I'm Lisa."

"Lisa. And what's brought you to these thick woods? The nearest ranger station is twenty miles away." The witch had long learned that it was easier to discover who they were while they could still speak. It made any visits from the sheriff or a search party member smoother to handle.

The girl responded eagerly, so many words spilling out that it soon grew obvious her true nature wasn't a solitary one despite her attempts to find the loneliest places. The witch hardly listened to the chatter, absorbing only key phrases. *Sabbatical. Looking for peace. Estranged family.*

She was already deciding the first cuts of meat to take when the girl said, "Are you out here on your own, too?"

Just as the witch swallowed a mouthful of drool to speak, a knock came at the door.

The girl turned to look, fingers still wringing out her snow-dampened hair. "Oh. That answers my question."

A knot of dread lodged itself in the witch's heart. She knew better than to believe two travelers could stumble upon her cabin at once. Knew better than to dismiss the way the shadows of the room darkened as the visitor on the other side of the door knocked once more.

"Come in," said the witch, trying to sound cheerful. "It's unlocked."

And then there he was, that devil creature, wearing his human form instead of his black fur. Oh, he looked innocent enough in his thick coat, worn jeans, and sturdy snow boots, but the witch already sensed the purpose of his visit and had to choke back a howl of rage.

"Came to patch the chinking, Franny." The wolf's gaze flickered over to the girl, as if he'd only just noticed her, before he added, "Sorry about interrupting things."

If she spoke, she wouldn't be able to keep from spitting at him. It didn't matter; the girl already smiled, eyes brightening. "It's all right. I thought Mrs. Harford was about to say that she's all alone out here. I'm glad she's got a friend after all."

"I like to keep an eye on things for her." The wolf's voice remained bland as he looked at the witch. She managed a smile, but her fingers curled into claws against the arms of her chair.

As the wolf went to work, patching the cracks between the logs where the wind whistled shrilly, the witch stared at the fire and trembled with rage. The girl stopped talking to her once the wolf promised to drive her back and dig her car free, instead chattering away at him even when his responses dwindled to brief glances.

If the witch still had any strength, she would have cursed the wolf's truck to break down, or glamored the girl's senses to keep her there. Instead, she was left to hiss at the fire when the door closed behind them, when an engine started up and rumbled away, leaving her entirely alone.

As night fell, one of her traps caught a rat as scrawny and desperate as herself, but the witch resisted biting into the raw meat. A mouthful of fur and bone might quell her stomach for a breath or two, but her rage demanded more. With a snarl, she ripped open the little body barehanded and plucked the heart free. Blood left her fingers slippery, but the witch had performed this summoning spell many times, and easily cast the lump of muscle into the thick of the flames.

As the fireplace brightened, she tossed a handful of herbs into it and muttered, "Come back here, you damned thing. You're as much a man as you are a wolf. Give in to your curiosity and come back here."

The smoke would travel for miles until it found him, combing through coarse fur or thick hair with invisible fingers to lure him back. Humans couldn't resist, and when the witch was at her full strength, neither could other creatures that lived in the shadows beyond the mundane world. But now she wasn't strong. Now she couldn't even call Ruth back to her. All the witch could do was wait and see if the wolf *would* come back and face her anger. Her stomach ached as she sucked her fingers clean.

The fire had dwindled to ashes and the moon hung high in the sky before he did, black fur stark against the snow-dusted ground. He skulked up the porch on rangy limbs before shifting form, unfazed by the chilly bite to the air.

"You and your damned softness toward women," she spat, sitting beside the heavy leather trunk she had wrestled down from the attic. "That girl would have kept me going for six months, maybe even a year."

"I took a look around yesterday. Someone's sending you money. You could buy food."

"Buy what? A piece of meat cut by another's knife and wrapped in sterile plastic? It's not the same and you know it. I need to take the life away. I need to hunt, much like you." Then the witch's face took on a hint of cunning. "But maybe... maybe we can reach a compromise."

She opened the heavy lid of the trunk, revealing a plush velvet interior. The wolf's eyes sharpened even before she withdrew a large pelt, its coarse fur still thick and full.

It was a wolf skin, each hair tipped gold from the final light of the flames.

"I made this from a beast that was already dead," said the witch, settling the pelt into her lap. "It took forever to pluck all the maggots and lice from the fur, but it's a fine thing now, isn't it?"

"It's dead skin," said the wolf, his voice revealing nothing of what he thought.

"True, true." Then the witch arranged it so that the toothlessness of the muzzle could be seen, so that the holes where the eyes had once been now peered at him. "How can I bring it back to life?"

The wolf's expression darkened.

The witch smiled in return. They always liked to think they were special, these creatures. That what they did couldn't be done by another. "You're an old one, aren't you? Far older than me. I'm sure you've heard of people wearing pelts to transform into creatures. I'm sure you've met some."

"I have." The green in the wolf's eyes had gone as flat as his voice. "And I can smell how you've already spelled the pelt to do the same for you."

"I did. Years ago, of course, when I was still strong. But it never worked for me, not even then."

The wolf suddenly smiled at her, a grim twitch of his lips that sent a chill through the witch's heart. "It can't. You're too empty. Always have been."

"What?" The witch's fingers curled against the fur.

When the wolf spoke again, she glimpsed his teeth and knew she was in for a savage bite. "Why did your daughter leave?"

"What a stupid question," she sniffed, dropping the pelt back in the trunk. "And one that I've already answered."

But the wolf's gaze didn't leave her face. "Why did she leave?"

"She lost the taste for this life. Went silly-headed over a boy and left." The words sounded hollow even to her.

"You used her as a lure for victims and she didn't like it."

"It's in her blood. There's no resisting your nature. *You* would know something about that, wouldn't you?"

If the words stung, he didn't show it. "I know your type. Always wanting to fill up the emptiness inside. Always gorging and feeling hungrier afterward. When you made that pelt, you ate the lice as you picked them free, didn't you? Even with a belly already full from the wolf's meat."

"Enough." The witch's mouth puckered shut.

Now the wolf glanced at the trunk. "You feed on everything. Rats, travelers... even your daughter was in danger.

If she ever came back, you'd hug her and then be gnawing on her bones by the next night."

"Enough!" A few grains of salt slid down the witch's cheeks. It was the closest she could come to crying.

"You called me, witch. I'm here."

For several breaths, silence fell between them. The wolf never looked away, eyes hot. Waiting.

"What will this boil down to, then?" she said, at last. "Me drawing people in and you chasing them away… we're two hunters in the same stretch of woods and neither of us can sate the other's appetite. Neither of us will stop and neither of us will win."

"We'll wait. Starve. See which of us lasts." Then the wolf flickered like a shadow, shifting into his other form.

As he shook his dark fur into place, the witch's voice trembled. "You think you'll weaken me, chasing them all away, but you're the desperate one."

Teeth flashed at her in a silent snarl before the wolf loped through the doorway, soon disappearing into the night.

The witch shrieked after him with salt tracks still on her face. "Look at you! Saving a few silly girls because you'll never find one who'll see your teeth without screaming. We're both sad things, wolf. I just admit it."

Eyes glowed at her from the dark of the woods, as bright as the moon that hung far above. Then they melted away in silence, leaving the witch to her hearth of ashes and her empty cooking pot.

About the Author

I've always loved writing about monsters and the girls who love them, which means I write a lot of werewolf romance. In my spare time I like to do things where I don't have to take myself seriously, like bike riding with my husband, baking anything that sounds good, and painting monsters and horses.

I like scotch, wine, and cats.

Enough about me; if you want to know more about my work, my personal website is juliemidnight.com, and my Instagram handle is @juliemidnighter